"Why do men a___ ____ ___
they're feeling?"

Gabriel glared at her, his arms rigid at his
sides. "Because talking doesn't always help."

"Then listen. Why are you beating yourself up
over something you had no control over?"

"Kinda like you?"

"You have a way of turning things around.
You're good at avoiding discussions of
yourself."

"Boring subject."

"Only to you."

"You think I'm interesting?"

"Yes. But then I think all my friends are
interesting or they wouldn't be my friends."

"Right. Friends."

"What do you want me to say? I'm not ready
for more, and all my energy has to be directed
at holding my family together."

"Then, I guess it's friends." He thrust his hand
toward her to shake.

"Yes," she declared in a strong voice, while
inside she felt as if she were lying to herself—
and him.

Books by Margaret Daley

Love Inspired

The Power of Love #168

MARGARET DALEY

feels she has been blessed. She has been married thirty-one years to Mike, whom she met in college. He is a terrific support and her best friend. They have one son, Shaun, who is marrying his high school sweetheart.

Margaret has been writing for many years and loves to tell a story. When she was a little girl, she would play with her dolls and make up stories about their lives. Now she writes these stories down. She especially enjoys weaving stories about families and how faith in God can sustain a person when things get tough. When she isn't writing, she is fortunate to be a teacher for students with special needs. She has taught for over twenty years and loves working with her students. She has also been a Special Olympics coach and participated in many sports with her students.

The Power of Love
Margaret Daley

Love Inspired®

Published by Steeple Hill Books™

STEEPLE HILL BOOKS

Steeple
Hill™

ISBN 0-373-87175-9

THE POWER OF LOVE

And we have known and believed the love that God hath to us. God is love; and he that dwelleth in love dwelleth in God, and God in him.

—*1 John* 4:16

This book is dedicated to the staff at Jenks High School and all the students I have had the privilege of teaching.

Chapter One

"What now?" Rebecca Michaels pulled back from the peephole, a frown marring her tired features.

When she opened her front door to the large policeman, tension whipped down her length. Standing next to the stranger was her son. The policeman's solemn expression told her the next few minutes wouldn't be a welcome-to-the-town exchange. She braced herself. "Is there something wrong, Officer?"

"Ma'am, is this your son?"

She nodded, her throat tightening.

"I found this young man behind the grocery store, loitering. He should be in school."

"That was where he was supposed to be." Rebecca directed her attention to her nine-year-old, whose features were set in a sullen expression. "What happened, Peter? You left an hour ago for school."

He dropped his gaze. "I didn't wanna go."

"That's not an option." Rebecca looked toward the policeman. "I'm sorry to have inconvenienced you. I'll make sure he gets to school when my baby wakes up."

The man stuck out his hand. "I'm Gabriel Stone. I haven't had the opportunity to welcome you to Oakview yet. Sorry it had to be this way."

Rebecca shook his hand, comforted by the firm feel of his fingers around hers. His handshake conveyed an impression of directness and no-nonsense that was refreshing. "I'm Rebecca Michaels." She relaxed the tense set of her shoulders.

"Well, ma'am, if you don't mind, I can take your son to school for you."

"I wouldn't want to put you out."

"No problem. That's part of my job, making sure the kids stay in school."

Grateful for his offer, she smiled. "Then great. My other son, Josh, just went down for a nap, and I hope he sleeps for a while."

The policeman returned her smile, the lines at the corners of his eyes deep as if he smiled a lot. "If you need any help, don't be a stranger. I live on the next block. I've known your grandmother for years."

As her son and Gabriel Stone turned to leave, Rebecca called, "Come right home after school, Peter. We need to talk."

The pout that graced her son's mouth made her wonder if she would have to go out looking for him after school. She started to say something further when Gabriel Stone said, "He'll be here. I'll make sure of that, ma'am."

Rebecca leaned against the doorjamb and watched her son and the policeman walk to the squad car. Gabriel Stone might bring Peter home this afternoon, but who was going to give her the strength to deal with this new problem? She squeezed her eyes closed and wished for the wisdom she would need to handle her eldest. He hadn't wanted to come to Oakview. He'd let her know that he hated his new school and wanted to go back to his old school in Dallas.

Had she made a wrong decision about coming to her grandmother's to live? She hadn't had much choice after her husband walked out on her and the children. Taking a deep breath of the spring-scented air, she relished the quiet of the moment, only the occasional sound of a bird in her grandmother's large oak tree breaking the silence.

"Rebecca, who was that?"

"Gabriel Stone." She closed the front door and turned toward her grandmother, who came from the back of the house, her cane tapping on the hardwood floor. She stopped, and with her shoulders hunched leaned on her cane, something she only did when she was really tired. Granny had been up part of the night with her and Josh. The doorbell must have awakened her. "Everything's okay. You should go back to sleep, Granny."

"I needed to get up. I never sleep past seven, and here it is nearly nine."

"You probably never stay up to all hours of the night, either. I'm sorry Josh was so fussy."

"My child, never apologize for that." Her grand-mother waved her hand toward the door. "I wish you

had asked Gabriel in for some coffee. I don't get to
see him nearly enough, especially now that he's the
new police chief.''

Police chief? She'd had no idea she had been talking to the person who ran Oakview's small police
department. He hadn't said a word. ''He'll be back
this afternoon.''

''Did he come over to welcome you to Oakview?
That would be just like the boy.''

''No.'' Rebecca wished that had been the case.
''Peter skipped school.''

''I knew he wasn't happy, but I never thought he
would do that.'' Rose Bennett headed for the kitchen.
''I think you could use a cup of coffee. You've been
up quite a while with Josh.''

Massaging the tight cords of her neck, Rebecca
followed her grandmother into the most cheerful
room in the house. Sunlight from a large bay window
bathed the kitchen. The yellow and powder-blue
flowered wallpaper, the white cabinets and the pol-
ished hardwood floors lent a warmth to the room that
Rebecca loved. She remembered spending a lot of
wonderful childhood days in this very kitchen, listening to her grandmother's stories of her family during the Oklahoma land rush. If she could, she would
spend most of her time in this room, cooking. She
rarely had that kind of time anymore.

Granny retrieved two mugs from the cabinet and
brought them to the pine table situated in front of the
bay window. ''Sit before you collapse. You look exhausted, my dear.''

Rebecca started to argue, then realized her grandmother was right. Weariness clung to every part of her. She could easily slump over on the table and go to sleep. She needed the caffeine to keep her awake so she could finish unpacking. Even though they'd been in Oakview for two weeks, they were still living in boxes. Peter would never feel as though this was his home as long as he had to get his things out of cardboard boxes. She was determined to have them settled completely as soon as possible. Then maybe they would begin to feel like a family again.

Granny poured coffee into the mugs, then took a seat next to Rebecca. "First, how's Josh? You must have finally managed to get him to sleep."

"You know Josh. He rarely complains. But his ears are still bothering him. He eventually went to sleep, I think out of pure exhaustion. I worry that his ear infection will spread to his lungs. You know the problems he can have with his breathing."

"He's such a sweet baby." Granny sipped her coffee. "Of course, I'm not sure he's considered a baby any longer. He'll be two soon. I wish I could help you more with him."

"Granny, offering to let us stay here has…" Rebecca swallowed hard, but the tears returned to plague her.

"Child, this is your home, too. Always will be." Rose patted Rebecca's hand. "You're family, and next to God, family is the most important thing in our lives."

"I wish Craig thought his family was important." Rebecca remembered a time when their small family had been important to Craig—before Josh was born.

When they had been first married, he'd wanted children, but over the years his feelings had changed.

Rose pinched her lips and snorted. "That man will regret leaving you one day, only by then it'll be too late."

"We've been divorced a year yesterday."

Rose placed her hand over Rebecca's. "I know, child. I'm sorry. With faith and time the pain will go away."

The feel of her grandmother's small, gnarled fingers over hers comforted Rebecca. "Time might help, but I don't know about faith, Granny. I think God stopped listening to my prayers long ago. I've tried so hard to keep this family together. My sons need…" She couldn't continue. The heartache of the past few years overwhelmed her, robbing her of her voice and capturing her breath in her lungs.

"It may seem that way, child, but He hasn't. He has a plan for you. You just don't know what it is yet." Rose squeezed Rebecca's hand. "You're here with me now. Things will start to look better."

Drawing in a shallow gulp of air, Rebecca swallowed past the tightness in her throat, determined to hold her family together somehow and reach her eldest son. "Peter's so miserable. He has never been openly hostile and defiant to me until lately. He used to love school. Now, I have to force him to go."

"Wait until he makes new friends. He'll forget all about Dallas."

Rebecca took several sips of her lukewarm coffee, wishing she had the faith that her grandmother had. When Craig had walked out on them eighteen months ago, she had prayed for help and guidance. None had come. Josh had to have surgery on his heart. The bills stacked up and Craig was slow to help pay for his children's upbringing. She had to sell the only home Peter had known and finally admit she couldn't make it in Dallas by herself. She'd returned to the town she'd grown up in Oklahoma.

Rebecca reached to pour herself another cup of coffee when she heard Josh's crying. Glancing at the time, she realized he hadn't slept more than half an hour. She pushed to her feet. "I'll see if I can't get him back to sleep."

Her grandmother caught her arm to stop her. "Honey, when God closes a door, He opens a window. Moving back to Oakview is a fresh start for you and your family. This is a wonderful town to raise your children in."

Rebecca leaned down and kissed her grandmother's wrinkled cheek. "If that's correct, then you're my window, and I appreciate you opening your home to me and my children. Ever since my parents died, you have been my anchor."

Josh continued to cry. Rebecca hurried upstairs to her bedroom, where he slept in a crib next to her bed. She looked at her youngest who had managed to turn over—finally, after twenty months. His face was beet red, and his short arms and legs were flailing.

"How's my little man?"

He turned his head toward her, his big brown eyes, slightly slanted at the corners, filled with tears.

"Nothing can be that bad," Rebecca said, scooping her son into her embrace. He fit in the cradle of her arms, his length no more than a one-year-old's.

Tears misted her eyes. Blinking them away, she began to sing Josh's favorite song. He cuddled against her, sleep slowly descending. She would not feel sorry for herself or Josh. That was wasted energy—energy she couldn't afford to waste.

Gabriel entered the clothing store and strode toward the elderly woman, sitting in an uncomfortable-looking chair with a young man standing over her with a scowl on his face.

When Ben Cross saw him approach, he waved his hand toward the white-haired woman and said, "I want her arrested. She tried to take a watch."

The elderly lady bristled. "Nonsense. I was admiring the watch, stuck it in my pocket to buy after I had looked around and forgot all about it."

"Ma'am—" Gabriel began.

"Bess Anderson. You can call me Bess, Officer. All my friends at the home do."

"Shady Oaks on First Street?"

"Why, yes. You know the place where I live?" She straightened her shoulders, clutching her purse handle with both hands.

The elderly woman reminded Gabriel of a typical grandmother of yesteryear. She was dressed in a floral print dress with sensible walking shoes and a felt hat on her head. All she was missing were white cotton gloves. "Ma'am, how—"

"Bess, please. Ma'am makes me sound so old, which I refuse to be."

"Bess, how did you get here?" Gabriel ignored the glares Ben was sending him.

"Why, I just walked out of the building and headed for town. I like to shop and haven't been in a while."

"Then let me take you home." Gabriel turned away from Bess and whispered to Ben, "I think this was all a misunderstanding. I'm inclined to accept her word that she just forgot about the watch being in her pocket. Is that okay with you?"

Ben pursed his lips, his eyes pinpoints.

"She's at least eighty. I can't see locking her up, Ben."

The young man sighed. "Okay. This time. This better not happen again."

Gabriel escorted Bess Anderson to his squad car. While the elderly woman gave him a rundown of her afternoon outing, he drove her the few blocks to the Shady Oaks Nursing Home. As he walked her toward the main building, the director came out the front door, worry carved into her expression.

"We've been looking all over the place for you, Bess. Is everything all right?"

"My goodness, yes. I just had a lovely stroll into town, and this nice gentleman offered to bring me home." Bess continued past the director.

Gabriel shook his head as he watched the old woman disappear into the building. "Bess Anderson is certainly an interesting character, Susan."

"And a handful. She's only been with us for a few weeks, and this is the second time she has walked away from the home. I don't know how she gets out.

Thank you for bringing her back. Do you want to come in for some tea? It's almost four. We were about to have it in the main lounge.''

''I'll take a rain check. I have a date with a young man at the school. In fact, if I don't get moving, I'll be late.''

Quickly Gabriel headed toward the elementary school. He pulled into a parking space just as the bell dismissed the children for the day. He climbed from the squad car and leaned against it, his arms folded across his chest, and waited for Peter Michaels to appear. Gabriel waved to several students coming out of the school, but he kept his gaze focused on the door. He wouldn't put it past the boy to try to sneak away. Peter hadn't been very happy this morning when Gabriel had deposited him in the principal's office before having a brief word with the man.

When the last student filed out of the school, Gabriel straightened and decided to head inside to see if Peter had given him the slip. He took two steps and stopped. Coming out of the building at a slow pace was the child in question. The sullen look on his face underscored the reluctance the boy felt.

Gabriel relaxed against the car and waited. He had a lot of patience, and he had a feeling he would need every bit of it to get through to Peter.

''Glad you could make it,'' Gabriel said, and opened his car door.

''This is dumb. I can walk home. It's only two blocks.''

''I told your mother I would give you a ride.''

The boy's frown deepened as he rounded the back of the sedan and climbed inside.

Gabriel started the engine and slanted a look toward Peter. He stared straight ahead, defiance stamped in his features. No small talk on this trip, Gabriel thought, and backed out of the parking space.

A few minutes later Gabriel pulled into Rose Bennett's driveway, and Peter jumped from the car before Gabriel could even switch off the engine. The boy raced for the house and disappeared inside so fast that Gabriel had to admire the child's quickness. He would be great on the baseball team. An idea formed and grew as Gabriel ambled to the house to pay his respects to Rose and maybe get to see Rebecca Michaels again.

All day he had been unable to shake the image of her wide eyes as she had stared at him. Deep in their blue depths he had glimpsed a vulnerability that touched him to the core. He hated to see someone hurting, and Rebecca was definitely in pain.

Even though Peter had left the front door open, Gabriel knocked on the screen, not wanting to ring the bell since her baby might be sleeping. He heard the sound of Rose's cane tapping against the floor as she shuffled toward him.

"My goodness, Gabriel, why are you standing out there? Come in. Are you through for the day?"

"Yes, ma'am."

"I just made a fresh pot of coffee, and I know how much you like my brew." Rose reached into the mailbox at the side of the door and retrieved several envelopes.

"No one makes it quite like you."

He stepped inside and glanced about him at the warmth of the house. Rose was determined to bring the outdoors inside. In every room there were vases of cut flowers from her garden and pots filled with green plants. The house's clean, fresh scent reminded him of a beautiful spring day.

"Now, that will definitely get you a second cup. I was in the kitchen trying to decide what to fix for dinner. Since Rebecca's moved in with her boys, we eat early. Why don't you stay and eat with us tonight?"

"I don't—"

Rose paused at the entrance to the kitchen, clasping both hands on the cane, her sharp, shrewd gaze directed at him. "I won't take no for an answer, son. I know for a fact you usually go home at night and eat by yourself in that big empty house of yours. Tonight you can eat with me and my family."

"Put that way, I can't refuse. I'll stay on one condition. You let me help with dinner." He enjoyed being a policeman in this Oklahoma town. The people had taken him into their hearts and made him feel a part of Oakview when he had moved here ten years before. They had comforted and shared in his pain, too. He would never forget their support.

"I'll let you share cleanup duty with my granddaughter. Cooking is one of my favorite things. Cleaning up isn't."

"It's a deal."

Gabriel sat at the kitchen table while Rose retrieved a blue mug from the cabinet and poured him some coffee. The aroma filled his nostrils, easing some of the day's tension. There was something in Peter's rebellious expression that concerned him, causing a warning to go off in his brain.

"I noticed you brought Peter home," Rose said, slipping a look at him while she stood at the stove and browned some ground beef. "Did he say anything to you?"

"Not a word."

"That's what I was afraid of. That child doesn't say much, and when he does he's always angry."

"Yep, that about sums up my experience with him." Gabriel took a long sip of his coffee, relishing the delicious taste of the rich brew as it slid down his throat.

"I've been trying to get him to church, but last Sunday I think he deliberately made himself throw up so he didn't have to go. I don't know what to do about him, and Rebecca is as lost as I am." Rose placed the wooden spoon on the counter and began cutting up an onion.

The aromas of cooking meat and fresh coffee reminded Gabriel of the home he used to have when his wife was alive. Now he usually heated up frozen dinners or grabbed something at the diner in town by the police station.

"What's he angry about?"

"He didn't want me to move to Oakview."

Gabriel peered over his shoulder at Rebecca, who stood in the doorway, that haunted look in her eyes again. His natural curiosity was aroused by this woman as he took in her petite build. Short brown hair framed an oval face, and her smooth, creamy complexion was devoid of any makeup. She wasn't beautiful, but there was something pleasing about her appearance.

"What did Peter say about skipping school?" Rose added the onion to the ground beef and stirred.

"Not much."

"Is Josh asleep finally?"

"Yes, but I don't know how long that will last. I hope the antibiotic takes effect soon."

"What's wrong?" Gabriel asked, finishing his coffee.

"An ear infection. Can I help, Granny?"

"No. I asked Gabriel to dinner, and he'll help you clean up. Sit and relax for a few minutes. You've been going a mile a minute since this morning."

Rebecca followed her grandmother's advice and took the chair at the opposite end of the kitchen table from Gabriel. Closing her eyes, she rolled her head and moved her shoulders. "Well, in between taking care of Josh, I did manage to empty a few more boxes. Only a dozen left."

Gabriel walked to the coffeepot and filled his mug. The scent of cooking onion saturated the air and made his stomach rumble. "Are you staying long?"

"I'm not sure what my plans are." She picked up the mail and flipped through the stack of letters.

"Did you receive your check?" Rose turned toward Rebecca, concern in her expression.

Frowning, Rebecca tossed the letters on the table. "No. He's late again. I don't know what I'm going to do."

"Is there something I can help you with?" Gabriel took the seat across from Rebecca, an urge to protect inundating him. In his line of work he often helped strangers, but this was different. He didn't like to see distress dull her eyes and wished he could erase it.

"No." Her gaze found his. "There isn't anything that you can do. My ex-husband is late with his child support. That's all." She shrugged as though it were nothing.

Gabriel seriously doubted it was that simple, but he saw the do-not-trespass sign go up and he didn't pursue the topic. Instead, he said, "I'd like to have Peter come out for the baseball team. I think he has potential."

"Baseball?"

"He's quick, and the guys on the team are a great bunch of kids. I help coach a Little League team after school."

"I doubt you'll get him to agree. All he wants to do lately is stay in his room and listen to music."

"Does he like music?"

"Yes."

"Maybe he could join the church choir. I'm the director. The children perform at the early service and the adults at the later one."

Rebecca stiffened, her jaw clenching. "You sound like a busy man. When do you have time for yourself?"

"Baseball and music are things I do for myself."

"Rebecca, you should see the children perform at church. Ever since Gabriel took over a few years back, the crowd of people attending our service has doubled. The choir is wonderful, and Gabriel's quite a singer. Rebecca used to be in her church's choir in Dallas.''

He dropped his gaze from Rebecca's face, feeling the heat of a blush tinge his cheeks. He had never been comfortable with compliments. Singing was a gift God had given him, and he wanted to share it with others, use it to spread His word. God had been his salvation when he had hit bottom after his wife and child died.

Gabriel shifted in his chair. ''We could always use another voice. Even if Peter doesn't want to sing, you're certainly welcome to join the adult choir.''

Rebecca came to her feet. Feelings of being rail-roaded into doing something she wasn't ready to han-dle overwhelmed her. She had forgotten about how small towns were. All she wanted to do was hide and lick her wounds. She was afraid people like Gabriel wouldn't allow her to. ''I think I hear Josh crying,'' she murmured and rushed from the room.

''I didn't hear anything,'' Gabriel said, frowning, not sure what had just happened.

Rose opened a can of kidney beans and one of tomatoes, then dumped the contents of both into the skillet. ''I guess I shouldn't have pushed. Rebecca's faith has been shaken ever since Craig left her. I know I'm supposed to forgive that man for what he did to my family, but I'm having a hard time. He walked out on Rebecca, Peter and Josh when they needed him the most. All he left her was a note on her pillow. She woke up one morning, and her marriage of twelve years was over." Rose snapped her fingers. "Just like that."

How could a man walk out on his family? Gabriel wondered, continually surprised by how easily some people discarded their children and wives when he would give anything to have a family. Memories of his loss engulfed him. Pain constricted his chest, making it difficult to breathe. In a few seconds, three years before, his whole life had been changed because a man had decided to drink and drive.

Gabriel started to say something when he heard footsteps approaching the kitchen. When Rebecca entered, she held a baby in her arms close to her chest. She placed the child in a swing set up in the corner, adjusted some tiny pillows to prop the boy up, then started it. When Gabriel saw Josh's features, he knew something was wrong.

Rebecca caught him staring at the child. "My son has Down's syndrome. His second birthday will be in six weeks, and yet he doesn't look a day over one."

Gabriel didn't know what to say to her announcement. She made it sound almost a challenge. Was the child the reason her husband had left? If so, how could he turn his back on one of God's creations? He would have given anything to be able to hold his own son, to cradle him to his chest. That wasn't possible, never would be.

"I hope you're planning a big party. Birthdays are important to children," Gabriel said, as though he was an expert on children when he had never really experienced the joys of fatherhood. His son had only lived a few hours. A tightness gripped his throat.

Rebecca went to the cabinet to get bowls. "I haven't thought that far ahead. I've been a little pre-occupied lately with the move and all." She heard the defensive tone in her voice and winced as she withdrew the bowls and closed the cabinet door.

"If you need any help—"

"No, I'm fine." She cut in, not wanting to hear his offer of assistance when she had never been able to get Craig even to change Josh's diaper. Again she experienced the stifling need to be alone to deal with the emotions threatening to overpower her. If it had been possible, she would have been better off staying in Dallas where she could get lost in a crowd.

"Rebecca!" Granny turned from the stove with the wooden spoon in her hand and a frown of dis-approval on her face.

Rebecca immediately regretted her cool interrup-tion. She attempted a smile that she knew didn't reach her eyes and said, "I'm sorry. It's been a long day."

"Go get Peter. Gabriel will set the table for us," her grandmother interjected.

Thankful to escape the kindness she glimpsed in Gabriel's dark eyes, she rushed from the kitchen and didn't slow her step until she was upstairs and out-side Peter's bedroom. Pausing, she inhaled a steady-ing breath, then knocked on his door.

All she heard coming from the room was the blare of music. She knocked again, louder.

The door swung open, and Peter scowled at her. "I'm not hungry."

"Then you don't have to eat. But you do have to come down to dinner and sit while we eat. We have a guest tonight."

"Who?"

"Chief Stone."

Her son set his mouth in a firm line. She didn't know if she had the strength to fight him if he refused to come downstairs. She did need help, but she was alone in this world except for her grandmother whom she didn't want to burden with her problems. Granny wasn't in the best of health, having suffered a mild stroke several years before.

Peter pushed past her and stomped down the stairs. Rebecca released her pent-up breath, then took a deep breath and blew it out through pursed lips. She needed to believe everything would work out, but each day she felt the weight on her shoulders growing.

Tears sprang into her eyes. She swiped at one that rolled down her cheek. She didn't have time to feel sorry for herself. Both Josh and Peter depended on her. Somehow she would hold this family together.

When she entered the kitchen and saw Gabriel sitting at the head of the kitchen table, she came to a halt inside the doorway. He looked at home, holding Josh, supporting his small body in the curve of his arm. Her heart slowed, then began to race at the sight of him smiling at her son. Josh smiled at Gabriel. The large, muscular man dwarfed her son, but the picture of the two of them seemed so right that Rebecca blinked as if she had been caught daydreaming the impossible.

For a few seconds Rebecca allowed herself to wonder how it would feel to have a man like Gabriel Stone supporting her emotionally, loving her children. She shook the thought from her mind. She could only depend on herself to keep this family together.

Chapter Two

"He wanted out of the swing when it stopped," Gabriel said, looking at her.

"Thank you for taking care of him," she murmured, retrieving her son from Gabriel and putting Josh into his high chair, again propping him with pillows so he could sit up. He was starting to support his weight, but he was still having trouble maintaining his balance for any length of time.

"There's a child in the church choir with Down's syndrome. He loves music."

"Josh does, too." Rebecca snapped on his bib.

Rose sat at the other end of the table, forcing Rebecca to take the chair next to Gabriel. "Let's join hands. Gabriel, will you give the blessing?"

Rebecca took Josh's tiny hand and Gabriel's larger one. The touch of Gabriel's fingers about hers sent warmth up her arm. The link felt natural and right. That surprised her.

"Heavenly Father, we come to this table to offer

our thanks for this wonderful food. Please watch over us and give us the strength to deal with our problems.''

The devotion in his voice gave Rebecca a sense of peace for the first time that day. She relished the blessing and wished she could feel that kind of love and faith again.

While Rose spooned chili into a bowl, then passed it to Peter, Rebecca fed Josh his baby food, mashed bananas and roast beef, two of his favorites. She introduced another food, strained carrots. He made a face and spit the carrots out. She dabbed at the orange that ran down his chin.

"Way to go, Josh. I hate carrots, too," Peter said, the first enthusiasm he had shown all day.

"So far, I haven't been able to find too many vegetables he likes." Rebecca tried another spoonful of carrots, which Josh immediately rejected.

"Have you tried mixing the bananas with the carrots and seeing if he'll eat that?" Gabriel set a chili bowl in front of Rebecca.

"Well, no. I suppose it wouldn't hurt." Rebecca dipped her spoon into the bananas and scooped some into the carrots. She wrinkled her nose at the mixture of light yellow and orange swirls.

When she fed Josh some of the new mixture, he kept most of it in his mouth. She gave him another spoonful, and he ate that, too.

"This might work with other vegetables, too. Thank you for the suggestion." Rebecca looked toward Gabriel.

His dark gaze caught hers and held it. "Anytime."

"Do you have any children?" she asked, realizing she knew nothing about this man and in many ways wished she did.

"No. Judy and I always wanted a whole house full." Pain flitted across his features for a few seconds before he managed to conceal his emotions.

"Judy is your wife?" Rebecca glimpsed a wedding ring on his left hand.

"She died three years ago." He touched his wedding ring, twisting it on his finger. "We had hoped to start a family when we moved here. It never happened."

"But he's determined to make up for that. He takes every child he can under his wing." Rose sipped water, her eyes twinkling.

Here was a man who had wanted children but didn't have any while her husband hadn't wanted to care for his two sons. Life wasn't fair, Rebecca thought, a constriction in her throat making it impossible to say another word. She dropped her gaze and continued to feed Josh.

A few minutes later Gabriel asked, "May I try that? You haven't had a chance to eat any of this great chili yet."

Rebecca hid her surprise at his request. She had always been the one to feed Josh. It was her responsibility, and she hadn't asked anyone else to do it. "I guess so."

"I've been watching you. I think I've got your technique down," he said with a sparkle in his dark brown eyes.

She blushed at the idea that he had been watching

what she'd been doing. The thought unnerved her more than she cared to think about.

"Eat while I finish up with this roast beef and banana-carrot combo."

Rebecca delved into the chili, filling her bowl with the delicious-smelling food. She was starved and hadn't realized it until she started eating. While she savored her meal, she watched Gabriel make a game of feeding her son. Josh smiled and cooed. Why couldn't this have been Craig enjoying his child?

"You know, Peter," Gabriel said while pretending to be a dive bomber coming in for a landing in Josh's mouth, "I noticed how fast you were running into the house. Have you ever thought about being on a baseball team?"

"Nope. I have better things to do after school."

"It does require a lot of time. It takes quite a commitment for a young man."

The challenge in Gabriel's voice dared Peter to accept. Her eldest straightened, his eyes becoming pinpoints. Peter didn't say anything, but he studied the police chief as though he wasn't quite sure what to make of the man.

At the end of the meal Gabriel wiped Josh's mouth. "Rose, that's the best food I've had in a long time. Thank you for inviting me to dinner."

"You're welcome." Rose gripped her cane and struggled to her feet. "Josh, Peter and I are going to retire to the living room while you two clean up. Peter, will you carry him for me?"

"Sure, Granny." Peter carefully picked up Josh

and followed his great-grandmother out of the room. "It's time for us to practice, Josh, my man."

Rebecca started taking dishes to the sink. "You don't have to help. I can take care of this mess if you need to leave."

"No. I told Rose I would help, and I always follow through on what I say." Gabriel brought several bowls and glasses to the counter.

While she rinsed the dishes, he put them into the dishwasher. They worked side by side in a silence that Rebecca didn't find awkward. A sense of teamwork eased any tension she experienced from his nearness. She usually felt the need to fill the void in a conversation with chitchat, but for some reason she didn't with Gabriel. Another surprise, she thought.

When she was through with the dishes, she noticed that it was dark outside the window over the sink. She reached to pull the shade down at the same time Gabriel turned toward her. Their arms grazed. Again that sense of warmth fanned from his touch. Startled by the brief contact, she flinched.

"Sorry. I didn't mean to bump into you," he said with a smile that crinkled the corners of his eyes, lending an appealing attraction to his tanned features.

"No problem." Rebecca yanked on the cord to lower the shade, then wrung out the washcloth to wipe the table and counters.

She felt Gabriel's gaze on her while she worked. The thought of him watching her made her heart beat faster. The silence between them hummed with alarming undercurrents. Her battered emotions were too raw for anything but friendship between them, if even that.

"I'm just about through in here if you want to go into the living room and join the others," she said, aware that her hands quivered.

He lounged against the counter, his stance casual, relaxed. "I'll wait. Can I help with anything else?"

She shook her head while she hurried the cleaning, the nape of her neck tingling where she imagined him staring.

"May I ask you a question?"

She pivoted toward him, clasping the edge of the kitchen table she had been wiping. Her legs felt weak, as though the strength had suddenly been siphoned from them. "Shoot." She laughed nervously. "Maybe I shouldn't say that to a policeman."

That warm smile of his touched his mouth again. "Josh doesn't just have Down's syndrome, he has something else wrong with him, doesn't he?"

Her grip tightened until her knuckles turned white. "Yes. He has spina bifida. His spine isn't developed. The doctors told me that he would never walk, talk or do anything."

"I'm sorry. That has to be hard on you."

Rebecca stared into his troubled gaze for a long moment, then shoved away from the table and draped the washcloth over the edge of the sink. "It's harder on Josh," she finally said as she headed for the living room.

She came to a stop in the doorway, aware that Gabriel was right behind her, looking over her shoulder. Peter clasped Josh under the arms and was helping him across the carpet. Tears returned to block her throat. Every night Peter practiced "walking" with Josh. Her oldest son was determined that Josh would one day play sports with him. That, according to the doctors, would never happen, and she didn't have the heart to tell Peter.

Gabriel set his hands on her shoulders and leaned close to whisper, "You're lucky to have such a nice family."

The wistful tone in his voice made Rebecca ache for what he must have lost when his wife died. His words helped her focus on what was right with her life. "Yes, thank you for reminding me of that."

When he dropped his hands, she immediately missed the warmth of his touch.

Through the fog of sleep, Rebecca heard the door-bell ringing. She dragged herself out of bed, slipped on her robe, then hurried to the front door. She peered out the peephole and saw Gabriel Stone. Why was he here at this hour? Then a thought struck her, and she quickly opened the door. Standing next to the police chief was Peter, for a second time in one day wearing a defiant expression on his face.

"Sorry to bother you at such a late hour, but I found your son running from a house that had just been egged."

"Whose house?"

"Mine."

"Peter Michaels, what do you have to say for yourself?"

Her son looked away, his frown deepening, his

mouth pinched as though he wouldn't say a word no matter what.

A chill swept her. Rebecca pulled her terry-cloth robe tighter about her and stepped to the side. "Please come in. I don't want to discuss this out on the porch for the whole town to hear."

Gabriel made sure that Peter entered the house before he came inside. "I'm willing to forget this incident. Since tomorrow's Saturday Peter can come by my house to clean up the mess."

"He'll be there. And when he's through cleaning up the eggs, he can do some other chores for you."

"I'll take care of my mess, but that's all." Peter crossed his arms over his chest, his features arranged in a stubborn expression.

Rebecca drew in a deep, bracing breath, so tired from no sleep and unpacking that all she wanted to do was collapse into a chair to have this discussion with her son. She gripped the banister, using it to support her weight. "That's not debatable." She looked toward Gabriel. "What time do you want us there?"

"Eight will be fine, if that's not too early for you."

"Are you kidding? I'm up at the crack of dawn with Josh."

"You can't make me!" Peter shouted, running up the stairs. "I won't go!"

Rebecca's first instinct was to hurry after her eldest, but when she heard his bedroom door slam shut, she winced and decided it wouldn't do any good. She might say something she would regret, because at the moment her patience was worn thin.

"I'm sorry, Rebecca. I hated to have to bring him home this way and at such an hour."

She shook her head. "You did the only thing you could. I didn't even know he was gone. He's never sneaked out before." She attempted a smile that she knew faltered. "At least not that I'm aware of. I'm afraid lately I don't know what my son is thinking or doing." She ran her hand through her hair, suddenly conscious of the fact that she must look a mess.

Gabriel smiled. "He'll come around when he gets used to Oakview. It's hard moving to a new town."

"We used to be very close until..." Rebecca couldn't finish the thought. She was tired of thinking about the past and what used to be.

"You don't have to come tomorrow morning. I'll make sure Peter does what he needs to do and I'll put him to work after he cleans up the eggs."

Rebecca straightened from the banister. "Peter's my problem, not yours. We'll be there tomorrow morning at eight sharp."

"If you need any help—"

"I appreciate the kind offer, but I'm fine." Rebecca walked to the front door and opened it.

Gabriel paused in the entrance and turned to say something but stopped when he saw her standing so proud and untouchable. She didn't know how to accept his help, and he wouldn't make things worse by saying anything else to her. She had enough to deal with. But it didn't stop his desire to wipe the sadness from her eyes.

He nodded, murmured, "Till tomorrow," and strode away from her house.

He climbed into the squad car and sat for a few minutes staring at a light in one of the upstairs bedrooms. The silence of the night soothed him, and he bowed his head. "Please, Lord, give me the guidance I need to help Rebecca and her children." He closed his eyes, drawing strength from the knowledge that He would be with him, that He would show him how to help Rebecca, Peter and Josh.

When Gabriel started the car, he felt calm, at peace as he always did after he communicated with God. He started to back out of the driveway when the radio sounded in the quiet. He responded to the call from the station, knowing it wouldn't be good.

"Stone here."

"There has been some vandalism at the school baseball field. Thought you might want to know, sir. I called your house, and when there wasn't an answer, I thought you might be out."

"Thanks, Bob. I'll head over there and take a look."

When Gabriel arrived at the baseball field, he immediately noticed the large window on the side of the main building was shattered. Taking his flashlight, he checked the area outside before shining the light through the smashed window, glass shards glittering on the concrete floor. Relieved to find the inside undisturbed, he headed for the front to have a closer look around. By the door he stepped on a broken egg in the gravel.

Peter Michaels. Of course, he had no proof the

damage had been done by the boy, but he would stake his career on it. Peter might not realize it, but Gabriel could tell when someone was crying out for help and he intended to give the boy that help, starting first thing tomorrow morning.

Rebecca pushed the bell again and heard its blare so she knew it was working. Suddenly the door jerked open, and she automatically stepped back. Gabriel with messed-up hair and a day's growth of beard greeted her with a puzzled look.

"What time is it?" he asked, combing his fingers through his conservatively styled black hair.

"Eight." She curled her fingers around the handle of the stroller that held Josh, staring at the overpowering man who had haphazardly dressed in a pair of jeans, a white T-shirt but no shoes.

Gabriel glanced at his watch. "I must have slept through my alarm. Sorry. Got to bed later than usual last night. There was a break-in at the baseball field." He directed his gaze toward Peter, who stood next to Rebecca.

She looked from the man to the boy, wondering if something was going on. Could Peter have been involved with the break-in? She hoped not, because if that was the case she had a bigger problem than her child not liking Oakview. "Peter, did you do anything else last night besides egg Chief Stone's house?"

The boy's bottom lip stuck out, and he stared at a point by his shoes. "What do you think I am? Stupid?"

"No. On the contrary, I think you're very smart,"
Rebecca replied, realizing her son hadn't answered
her question. From his expression she also realized
she wouldn't get an answer out of him.

"Come inside while I put some coffee on. I have
to have at least a cup before I can start functioning
in the morning." Gabriel moved to allow them entrance into his home.

Rebecca hesitated. She had only come with Peter
to make sure he showed up. After a confrontation in
his bedroom, she couldn't be sure of anything with
her son.

"My coffee isn't as good as Rose's, but it's not
too bad." Gabriel waved them inside.

Rebecca picked up Josh and followed Peter into
the house, trying to dismiss her eldest son's anger.
When she'd grounded him for shouting at her earlier,
he had laughed as though what she had said meant
nothing to him.

"Have you all had breakfast?"

"Granny won't let anyone leave without a proper
start to the day, as she refers to breakfast." Rebecca
held Josh close, comforted by his presence.

"Has she fixed you her cinnamon rolls yet?"

"Last Sunday. When I woke up, the house smelled
of cinnamon and baking bread."

"What a wonderful way to start the Lord's day."

Rebecca glanced around at the house as she
walked toward the back. His living room looked
comfortable, with a navy and burgundy plaid couch,
large pillows and stacks of magazines and books. She
pictured him stretched out in his navy blue recliner,

reading a book while a fire blazed in the fireplace and soft music played in the background. His home reflected the man, comfortable and laid-back.

"Have a seat while I put the coffee on."

Rebecca settled herself at the kitchen table, made of sturdy oak with enough chairs to seat a family of six. She placed Josh on her lap, pleased to see her youngest son show interest in his surroundings. Light streamed through the large window over the sink. She smiled, thinking it was appropriate for a lawman to decorate in red, white and blue.

Peter remained by the doorway into the kitchen, such anger on his face that Gabriel wished again for a magic answer on how to help the Michaels family. *Keep the faith. God has His own timetable,* he reminded himself as he sat across from Rebecca. *The answer will come when the time is right.*

"If you want to get started on the cleanup, Peter, I have a bucket and a scrub brush in the garage through there." Gabriel pointed toward a utility room.

Peter shot Gabriel a look full of anger, then stomped toward the garage, muttering something that Gabriel was glad he wasn't privy to. There was a limit to every person's patience, and with Peter he was afraid he would need an extra dose.

Gabriel looked at Rebecca, who was watching her son leave. The sadness in her eyes contracted his heart. "Physical labor will help him get rid of some of that hostility."

While her gaze connected with Gabriel's, Rebecca

hugged Josh closer, as though he could shield her from heartache. "He's so full of anger. I've tried talking to him about it, but he won't say anything." Again the scene in her son's bedroom swamped her with feelings of inadequacy. Peter was a different child from the year before.

"Have you tried counseling?"

"Yes. He just sat there, determined not to say a word to the woman."

"How about the minister of your church?"

Rebecca shook her head.

"Ours is very good with young people."

"No." She answered so quickly she surprised even herself. "I'm sure he wouldn't respond to a stranger," she offered in explanation.

Gabriel noticed the firm set to Rebecca's mouth, the tension transmitted in the rigid lines of her body, and knew she would reject any coaxing to get Peter or herself to talk with Reverend Carson. "Then let me try to help."

"I can't accept—"

Gabriel held up his hand to stop her flow of words. "I'm worried about Peter. I think he might have vandalized the baseball-field house. I found a broken egg by the front door. I don't believe in coincidences."

Rebecca closed her eyes for a few seconds. She adjusted Josh in her arms and kissed the top of his head, drawing strength from her youngest. "He might be innocent. You don't know he did anything."

"What do you think in your heart?"

She rubbed her cheek against Josh's hair, then

peered at Gabriel, her eyes glistening. "What do I do?"

"Let me help. I've dealt with troubled children before, and not as a lawman."

Again she shifted Josh in her arms, looking away from Gabriel.

"May I hold Josh?" The need to hold the child ran deep in him. Gabriel had missed so much with his own son.

Her gaze returned to his, confusion deep in her eyes. She hesitated, then rose and handed Gabriel her child. Josh's big brown eyes focused on his face. A tightness threatened to close his throat as he stared at the small boy in his embrace. He supported Josh in the crook of his arm. Smiling at him, Gabriel found himself making silly faces to get the child to grin. And when Josh did, Gabriel's heart swelled with pride.

"How are his ears today?"

"Last night he slept through the night for the first time in several weeks. I think the medicine is finally working. At least I hope so."

Gabriel tore his gaze from the child and looked at Josh's mother. Holding Josh only underscored for Gabriel what he was missing. The emptiness inside pushed to the foreground.

"So do I. It's not easy going without sleep," he finally said, realizing an awkward silence had descended.

She sighed. "Something I'm quickly finding out."

"What are your plans now that you've moved to

Oakview?'' He had dealt with his loss and didn't want to renew the feelings of anguish.

''I need to get a job soon.''

''You know I might be able to help you with that.''

A closed expression settled over Rebecca's features. ''You've already done enough.''

''Nonsense. What are friends for? Let me ask around. What are your qualifications?''

When she laughed, there was no humor in the sound. ''I don't have any.''

''Everyone has qualifications.''

''I've been a mother and wife for the past ten years. I suppose I can clean houses, chauffeur and organize PTA meetings.'' She snapped her fingers. ''Oh, and I have some computer skills. We had one at home.''

''What will you do with Josh when you go to work?''

She cocked her head. ''Frankly, I don't know. I can't keep staying at Granny's house and not contribute to the finances.''

''I'm finished. Can we go now?'' Peter announced from the doorway into the utility room.

''You still owe me some of your time.''

Peter folded his arms. ''How much?''

''I'll take you home in the early afternoon.'' Gabriel glanced at Rebecca to make sure that was all right with her.

She nodded, then stood to take Josh from Gabriel. ''We'd better be going. I want Josh to take a nap in his own crib.''

"I have baseball practice this afternoon, so Peter should be home by two. I'll feed him lunch."

"Fine," she mumbled as she started for the door. When Gabriel rose to escort her, she added, "I can find my own way out. Finish your coffee."

Peering at his mug, he realized he hadn't taken a sip of his cold coffee. He dumped the brew into the sink and poured some more into his cup, steamy whiffs of the hot liquid wafting to him.

"What do I have to do?" Peter asked in a surly voice.

Gabriel brought the mug to his lips and took a long sip of the coffee, purposefully waiting a good minute to answer the boy. "This is my Saturday to do yard work at the church. You're going to help me."

Peter opened his mouth to reply, then snapped his jaws together, his teeth making a clicking sound.

"Why don't you go check on Lady out back?"

"Lady?"

"My dog. She has puppies. See if there's enough water for them while I get ready." Gabriel watched the child stalk to the back door and yank it open, anger in every line of the boy's body. The next few hours could be very long.

"Peter, this is David Carson. He's going to help us." Gabriel opened the door to the church's shed and went inside.

"You're the new kid at school," David said with a wide grin.

"Yeah. What of it?"

David's smile vanished. "Nothing. Just making conversation."

Gabriel heard the wonderful start to the exchange between the two boys and wasn't so sure it was a good idea to have David here helping. He had thought introducing Peter to some nice kids his age would make the situation easier.

Gabriel handed David a plastic lawn bag. "First, we need to pick up any trash, then pull weeds in the gardens."

Peter crossed his arms and refused to take the bag Gabriel held for him. "I don't pick up trash."

"There's a first time for everything." Gabriel stood his ground.

Peter narrowed his eyes and stuck out his lower lip. Then when Gabriel thought Peter would run away, he yanked the bag from Gabriel's hand and stomped off toward the nearest garden.

"What's his problem?" David asked, jerking his right thumb toward Peter.

Gabriel watched Peter yank up a plant that wasn't a weed. "He needs a friend. I thought you might help me out there."

David's eyes grew round. "Are you sure? At school he isn't very friendly. Keeps to himself."

Gabriel clasped David on the shoulder. "You've grown up here. Everyone is familiar to you. What do you think it would be like if that wasn't the case?"

"I guess, scary."

"My point exactly." Gabriel squeezed David's shoulder briefly, then added, "Let's go see if we can save some of the plants."

Two hours later Gabriel stepped back to inspect their work, pleased. He had managed to save most of the plants, and the gardens looked great. He took pride in maintaining these beds as though it was his statement about the glory of God to the world. The flowers showcased the beauty He was capable of.

"Let's take a break and go inside to get some sodas." Gabriel took the plastic bags from the two boys.

David headed for the door. Peter stared at the church, hesitating.

"I'll stay and do some more work," Peter said as Gabriel started to follow David.

"Even God declared a day of rest. You worked hard. You deserve a break."

Peter blinked as though Gabriel's words surprised him.

"He welcomes everyone into His house." Gabriel walked toward the church, hoping that the child would join David and him. But he knew he couldn't force Peter. He had to want to come inside the Lord's house.

Gabriel selected a soft drink after David, then propped himself against the wall and sipped his soda. His disappointment grew as the minutes ticked by and Peter didn't appear.

Gabriel had half finished his soft drink when Peter shuffled into the alcove outside the large meeting room. "What do you want to drink?"

Peter scanned the choices in the machine. His eyes lit up for a few seconds. "Strawberry cream soda."

"Hey, that's my favorite. No one else at school likes it." David tipped up his can and emptied it.

"They just don't know a great drink when they see it." Peter took the can from Gabriel, then moved back, keeping his distance.

"This is probably the only vending machine in town with strawberry cream sodas. Dad keeps it stocked for me."

"Dad?"

"He's the minister here."

"Oh. Isn't that kinda hard on you?" Peter asked as though it were a disease to have a father be a minister.

David laughed. "Nah. Dad's pretty cool about things."

Peter tipped the can to his mouth and nearly drained it in one long swallow. "Mmm. I haven't had one of these in a while. Mom couldn't find it at the grocery store last week."

"Now you know where to come if you ever run out at home. The church is always open." Gabriel tossed his empty can into the trash. "Ready to get back to work?"

"Sure. We've got baseball practice later today, and our coach is a real stickler for being on time." David slid a glance toward Gabriel, then crushed his can and aimed for the trash bin several feet away. The can landed in the container. "Yes! I haven't lost my touch since basketball season."

Peter frowned. "You play a lot of sports?"

"Yeah. You should come out for the baseball team."

"I don't play baseball." Peter dropped his can into the trash and shuffled out of the alcove ahead of Gabriel and David.

When Gabriel stepped outside, he said, "That offer to come out for the team still stands. We take newcomers all the time." He knew he was taking a risk by extending the invitation again. He didn't particularly want to spend another late night cleaning up the field house.

"Yeah, we need someone who's fast," David said, hurrying to catch up with Peter.

"I don't run, either." Peter came to a halt in front of the shed, his frown firmly in place.

"I've seen you in gym class. You're fast. Even our teacher said something about that the other day."

Peter slanted a look toward David. A thoughtful expression replaced Peter's frown. "Nah. She just wanted to make me feel welcome." He dug the toe of his shoe into the dirt.

"Not Mrs. Hinds. She loves to point out a kid's bad points. She's the regular terror of our school."

Peter laughed. "Yeah, I kinda figured that the first day."

Gabriel walked into the shed while the boys discussed the gym teacher who had been at the school thirty years, prodding children who preferred to sit in front of a television into exercising. Hearing Peter's laughter firmed his resolve to help the boy. He again said a silent prayer for assistance.

Several hours later, at the local diner, Gabriel and the boys ate hamburgers and fries. After their lunch Gabriel took David home, then Peter. As Gabriel pulled into the driveway, he saw Rebecca sitting on the porch swing and couldn't resist the urge to say a few words to her.

As he approached, he noticed Rebecca's brow knitted in worry, her hands clutching a letter. He wanted to ask her if he could help, but remembered her reaction when he had. She felt she had to struggle alone.

"Something wrong?"

Rebecca lifted her head, squeezing her eyes closed for a few seconds. Seeing the sheen of tears, he fought the urge to hold her close.

She swallowed several times, then looked toward him. "An overdue bill from the hospital."

Gabriel eased beside her on the porch swing. He remained quiet, allowing her to set the pace and tone of the conversation.

"You know, I tried to explain to them that I'll pay when I can. You can't get blood out of a turnip. It's not like I don't put something toward the bill each month." She shrugged, trying to smile but failing. "I guess they didn't like the small amount this month. I need a job *now*."

"If I hear of anything, I'll let you know right away. Of course, since this is a small town, you might have to go to Tulsa to look for a job."

"I know. I hope not." She balled the bill in her hand. "How did Peter do?"

"Not bad. He enjoyed playing with my mutt, Lady. She has three puppies that are all over the place. He was in the midst of them when I went out back to get him."

"Craig would never let Peter have a pet."

The more he heard about Rebecca's ex-husband, the more he was glad the man didn't live in Oakview. Gabriel was afraid the man would test his faith. Some people didn't know how to appreciate what God had given them. "After a rocky start, Peter and David Carson got along pretty good."

"I'm glad to hear that. If Peter could make a friend, I think that'll help his adjustment."

"That's the plan."

With her head tilted, she stared at him. "Thank you. I appreciate the help."

Gabriel realized her admission had been difficult, and that made it all the more special. He smiled, pleased to see her return it, her eyes sparkling with a vivid blue. He was determined to show her she wasn't alone, that God was with her, and if she would accept him, he was too.

Chapter Three

"Well, my man, I hope you're ready for bed because your mother sure is. These late nights are killers," Rebecca said, picking Josh up and cradling him close.

She sat in the chair by the crib and began to rock. After she'd sung two lullabies, Josh closed his eyes and relaxed.

Rebecca heard her grandmother approaching the bedroom. She looked up to find Granny standing in the doorway. "I hope my singing didn't awaken you."

"Never. I love hearing you sing. I had to go to the bathroom, heard you up and thought I would check to see if Josh was asleep yet."

"Yes." Rebecca pushed to her feet and carefully laid her son in his crib. "I think tonight he'll sleep through to morning once again. At least I hope so." She came into the hallway.

"Peter didn't say anything at dinner about going to Gabriel's. Did he say anything afterwards?"

"He said something about a dog with puppies, then grumbled about pulling weeds at the church. That's all I got out of him." Rebecca sighed, remembering the one-word answers she had received from her eldest at the dinner table. The only time he had been a part of the family that day was when he had worked with Josh after supper.

"I'm glad he was at the church today. Gabriel usually works there on Saturdays, along with some of the young people. I hope Peter met some kids he could be friends with. That's what he needs, church and friends."

"He needs a father who will care about him. Craig hasn't called him in the two weeks we have been here. His birthday is coming up, and I know Peter will want his dad here to help him celebrate. What should I do?"

"Have you talked with Craig lately?"

"No, not since our move."

"Call him and let him know the importance of Peter's birthday to the child."

Rebecca rolled her shoulders and kneaded the tight cords of her neck. "I'm not sure my call would help the situation, but I'll try." She started for Peter's bedroom. "Peter's been unusually quiet this evening. No loud music from his room."

Rebecca opened the door and peered into the darkened bedroom. The window was up, allowing a soft breeze to stir the curtains, the scent of the outdoors to fill the room. A shaft of moonlight streamed through the opening and across Peter's empty bed.

"He's not here." Rebecca flipped on the overhead light and scanned the area. "Oh, no. He sneaked out again."

"He might be downstairs. Check the house first before you get too upset."

Rebecca inhaled deeply, but nothing alleviated the tension building inside. "You're probably right. He's downstairs watching television as we speak."

She made her way to the first floor and went from room to room. Finally, ten minutes later, she had to acknowledge that Peter wasn't in the house. She checked the front porch then the yard, and there was no sign of her son.

Granny appeared in the kitchen. "Gone?"

Rebecca nodded, her throat tight with suppressed emotion. She was scared. What kind of trouble was her eldest getting into at this very moment? Where was he? She sank onto a chair and buried her face in her hands. She felt so alone.

Her grandmother put her hand on Rebecca's shoulder. "Call Gabriel. He'll help."

She remembered Gabriel's suspicion about Peter vandalizing the field house. "But he's the police chief. What if—" Rebecca couldn't voice her fear that Peter was getting into trouble, the kind of trouble the law would be interested in.

"Gabriel is a friend of this family. Ask him to help."

She hated asking anyone for help, but fear compelled her to reach for the phone. Her hands trembling, Rebecca dialed the police chief's number. In less than twenty-four hours this man had become part of her new life.

Gabriel climbed into his squad car and gripped the steering wheel. Staring out the windshield, he tried to come up with another place Peter might go. The boy hadn't been at the usual hangouts or behind the store where Gabriel had first seen him.

Gabriel closed his eyes and bowed his head. "Dear Lord, please help me find Peter. He's hurting, and I want to help."

As he turned the key in the ignition, he suddenly knew where to find Rebecca's son. He backed out of the parking space at the rodeo grounds and headed for the high school baseball field. When he pulled into the lot next to the stands, he saw someone sitting in the bleachers, his head buried in his hands, the slump of his shoulders emphasizing his dejection.

Gabriel switched off his headlights and quietly climbed the stands. He hung back until his eyes adjusted to the dark and he could see who the person was. Relieved at finally finding the boy, Gabriel made his way toward Peter.

Gabriel hated sneaking up on someone but knew the boy would run if given the chance. He laid his hand on Peter's shoulder. The child gasped and turned.

"Easy, Peter. It's just me, Chief Stone." He kept his voice even, calm.

Peter started scrambling away. Gabriel's grip on his shoulder strengthened.

"Leave me alone. I didn't do anything wrong."

"Well, for starters, son, you're trespassing."

"I'm not your son!" Peter twisted and finally managed to slip from Gabriel's grasp.

The defensive anger in Peter's voice tore at Gabriel. "Don't make this any worse. Come on. Let's go to my car."

"No! I didn't do anything wrong," Peter shouted, so loudly Gabriel was sure the people who lived nearby heard him. "This baseball field belongs to the public, and I am part of the public."

Gabriel decided to change tactics. "Okay. If you want to stay, I'll stay." He sat down and waited, resting his elbows on his knees and loosely clasping his hands.

In the dim moonlight Gabriel saw the boy's mouth twist into a deep frown, his hands clenching and unclenching at his sides. Finally Peter took a seat and tried to ignore Gabriel. That was all right with him. He knew dealing with Peter would call upon his patience, and thankfully God had given him a huge reserve. Peter slumped and rested his chin in his palms.

"Your mom's worried about you," Gabriel said a few minutes later.

Peter stiffened, bringing his head up.

"Don't you think we should at least give her a call and let her know you're all right?"

"She doesn't care about me."

"Well, she certainly had me fooled earlier on the phone. I could have sworn I heard her crying."

Peter remained silent, leaning forward, his chin on

his fist, as though settling in for the night. He fixed his gaze on the baseball field, illuminated by the three-quarter moon.

Gabriel retrieved his cell phone from his shirt pocket and dialed Rebecca's number. "Peter's okay," he said when Rebecca answered on the first ring, and quickly filled her in on where he'd found Peter.

There was a moment's hesitation, then she asked, "Is there—did he cause any problems?"

"No," Gabriel said, not sure if Peter had vandalized the field house or not. His brief inspection on his way to the stands had revealed nothing wrong. "I'll bring him home soon."

"Thank you, Gabriel. I don't…" Her voice trailed into silence.

"You're welcome, Rebecca. Peter and I will see you in a while."

"Is she mad?"

Gabriel remembered the silence at the end, a vulnerable pause in her sentence while she tried to gather her composure. "She's more worried than anything."

"She's always worried."

"What about?" Gabriel asked, wanting to keep the fragile conversation going but realizing he wanted to know so much more about Rebecca Michaels than he did.

"Josh, Granny, money—me."

"I find that moms worry a lot. I think that's part of being a mother. Mine still worries about me, and

I'm thirty-six years old and have been away from home for seventeen years.''

"Yeah, well, I can take care of myself. I don't need nobody to worry about me.''

Gabriel smiled at Peter's tough-sounding voice and remembered once there had been a time he'd thought the same thing. God had proven him wrong. God had shown him he wasn't alone in this world.

"Even when you're able to take care of yourself, it's nice to know someone is there for you.''

"I don't need nobody,'' Peter said, the strength in his voice lessening slightly.

For a brief moment Gabriel felt himself hurled back twenty years. He had declared that same thing to his mother after his father had died, leaving him the man of the house with three younger siblings. In his anger he had nearly lost his way until his grandfather had shown him the power of the Lord's love. That power had been strengthened when Gabriel had lost his wife and son—a son who wouldn't be much older than Josh. Emotions he thought were behind him surfaced, knotting his throat. He had so wanted a family.

"It can get mighty lonely going through life by yourself,'' Gabriel finally said, twisting his wedding ring as memories of the day Judy had slid it on his finger seeped into his thoughts. He had never taken it off.

"But at least no one can let—'' Peter snapped his mouth closed.

"Let you down?''

In the moonlight Peter tensed, his jaw clamped tight.

"Who let you down, Peter?"

"Nobody!" Peter shot to his feet. "I can find my own way home."

Gabriel rose. "No, I told your mother I would bring you home, and I'm going to do what I promised. You'll find that I always do."

"Fine!" The child shoved past him and hastened to the squad car.

Gabriel peered heavenward, noting the clear sky, the stars glittering in the blackness. The spring air was warm, the light breeze carrying a hint of honeysuckle. Perfect—except for the storm brewing at the Michaels's house. He felt Peter's anger as though it were a palpable force, reaching out to push everyone away. The child was determined to stand alone no matter who got in his way.

When Gabriel slid behind the steering wheel, he turned to Peter and asked, "Why did you come to the field tonight?"

The boy shrugged.

"Have you been thinking about my offer to join the team?"

"No way." Peter answered so fast Gabriel knew the opposite was true.

"If you don't want to play, I could use an assistant."

"I'm sure I won't be able to do anything for a while. Mom's gonna ground me longer for leaving the house. I'll probably not be able to do anything till summer."

"Then why did you do it?"

"'Cause I felt like it."

Gabriel heard the pout and stubbornness in the child's voice and again thought of how he had been after his father's death, so angry at the world. "What if I can get your mother to let you come out for the team?"

"Sure, why not. It beats staying in that old house. But I ain't gonna play."

Gabriel started the car, careful to keep from grinning. Once he had Peter at the baseball field, he would get the boy involved in the team as more than an assistant. Of course, he had to convince Rebecca to allow Peter to practice after school. Normally he wouldn't think that was a problem, but with Rebecca, he didn't know what to expect.

Rebecca answered the door on the first knock, throwing her arms around Peter's stiff body and pulling him against her. "Don't ever scare me like that again." She stood him away from her and inspected him as though afraid he had been hurt. "Why did you leave?"

Her son shuffled back a few steps and looked at his feet. "I needed some fresh air." He lifted his head and fixed his gaze on her.

Rebecca wanted to shake some sense into him but knew anger wouldn't bring about the peace she so desperately needed. She balled her hands at her sides and counted to ten. When she still wasn't calm, she started for one hundred. "We'll talk about this in the morning."

Peter's chin went up a notch. "Why not now? You're just gonna ground me."

Her fingernails dug into her palms. "I don't know what I'm going to do. I do know that I need to calm down first or I might regret what I say."

"Tell him—" Peter nodded toward Gabriel "—that I'm grounded and won't be able to help with the baseball team after school."

"Why, that's a great idea, Peter. You should become involved with a sport."

"Oh, good grief." Her son tramped across the entrance hall.

"Peter, I'll see you Monday right after school at the field. Wear your tennis shoes," Gabriel called as the boy fled up the stairs.

At the top her son stopped. "I might be busy. Mrs. Harris wants to see me."

"Then come as soon as you can."

Peter frowned, started to say something else, then stalked toward his bedroom.

"Mrs. Harris wants to see him?" Rebecca stared at the place her son had been standing. "That's the first I heard of it. Of course, that doesn't surprise me. Lately, there's a lot I don't know about my son. We used to be so close." She massaged the muscles in her neck and shoulders to ease the tightness. "I can't believe you talked Peter into going out for the baseball team."

"I didn't, exactly. He's going to be my assistant."

"Assistant? That's even more of a surprise."

Gabriel chuckled. "I sort of backed him into a corner."

Rebecca slanted another look up the stairs, her heart beating normally again. Her vivid imagination had conjured up all kinds of trouble for Peter. "Did he say anything to you about why he left the house?"

"No, not exactly. For a second I thought he was going to tell me about someone letting him down."

"No doubt me for moving here."

"I think it's someone else. Talk to him tomorrow. Maybe he will be ready to tell you."

"Maybe," she murmured, knowing in her heart that her eldest wouldn't talk to her about what was troubling him. In the past year their relationship had unraveled, and she didn't know how to stop it from coming completely apart. "Thanks again for all your help."

"It's part of my job. I'm just glad it ended okay."

"Yeah, but you've lost several nights of sleep because of my family."

"I wasn't in bed yet. I was trying to read a book and not getting very far." He started to turn away and stopped. "I was going to call you anyway tomorrow."

"You were?"

"Jenny, our file clerk at the station, decided to elope last night. I got a call from her late this afternoon. She and her new husband are going to live in Oklahoma City. We could use a new file clerk, sometimes a dispatcher. It doesn't pay much, but I hope you'll apply."

"File clerk? I think I can handle that."

"There's some computer work involved, too."

"That shouldn't be a problem. If I don't know

your programs, I should be able to pick it up quickly.''

A smile flashed across his face. ''Then call the station and set up an interview with my secretary, Mabel.''

Rebecca watched Gabriel stroll away, both elated and apprehensive. With a job on the horizon, she had to work out child care for Josh. She didn't want to leave him, and yet she had to earn some money to support her family, to pay the bills. Craig wasn't reliable, and Josh's care was expensive. If she got the job at the police station, at least she would be staying in Oakview. As she closed the front door, she pushed her doubts to the background and made a promise to herself. Gabriel Stone would not regret giving her this chance.

Chapter Four

Rebecca heard the back door slam. Peering into the kitchen, she saw Peter go to the refrigerator. He took a jug of ice water out and poured himself a tall glass.

"How was practice today?" Rebecca came into the room, hoping that her son would finally say more than two words to her. She'd never had the talk with Peter because he'd avoided her, and she knew the uselessness of having a conversation with him when he was in a rotten mood.

"Just great," he mumbled. "One of my favorite things is to run laps around a baseball diamond." The frown carved into his features belied his words.

"I thought you were the assistant."

"Yeah, well, it seems the assistant runs along with everyone else, even the coaches. Something that Coach Stone forgot to tell me the other night."

"I guess you couldn't very well stand there watching everyone run."

"Right, and he knew that I'd feel awkward." Peter's frown deepened as he trudged to the sink and put his glass in it.

Rebecca looked at her son's dress shoes. "Where are your sneakers? You didn't run in those, did you?"

"Yes." Peter stared at the sink as though he had never seen it before. "I forgot them, but *he* didn't believe me. He made me run anyway."

"Did you really forget them?"

Peter whirled. "Yes, of course!"

"But you never wear your dress shoes to school."

"Well, I wanted to today." He glared at her, daring her to disagree.

"Let's talk, Peter."

"Now? I'm beat."

"Then have a seat at the table." Rebecca gestured toward it. "We've put this off too long. We need to talk about Saturday night." She made her voice firm, no-nonsense sounding.

Peter loudly sighed but walked to the table and plopped into a chair, slouching against its caned back.

"Chief Stone thinks that you're upset because you feel someone has let you down."

"He should mind his own business," Peter mumbled, picking at the bright yellow place mat in front of him.

"Lately you have been his business. When you disappeared the other night, you became his business."

"Only because you called him." He stabbed her with a defiant glare.

"I was afraid something bad would happen to you. Nine-year-old boys don't go out at midnight."

"I'm gonna be ten soon." Peter dropped his gaze and began to roll the place mat at the corner.

"Ten-year-old boys don't, either."

"I'm not a baby anymore."

Rebecca grasped his hand. "I know that. Both Josh and I depend on you, honey. That's why I can't have you leaving the house late at night. I don't know what I would do without you." Emotion welled in her throat.

Peter kept his head down, his shoulders slumped.

"Promise me you won't do that again."

He mumbled what she thought was a yes.

"And as long as you're involved with the baseball team, I won't extend your grounding. I think it's important you do something like that." She realized the second she said those words that she might be dooming Peter's participation with the team. Lately he seemed to go out of his way not to do what she wanted. "Now, speaking of your birthday, what do you want to do for it? We could have a party and invite—"

Peter's head shot up, and he yanked his hand from her clasp. "I don't know anyone in Oakview to invite. All of my friends are back in Dallas."

"Then what do you want to do?"

Chewing on his lower lip, he glanced away then at her. "I want to go fishing with Dad like we used to."

The tightness in her throat spread. Her lungs burned. Craig and Peter used to go fishing at least once a month. Her son loved to fish and hadn't been since Craig had left them. "Then we'll call him and see what we can set up."

His face brightened. "We can?"

"Yes, let's call this evening after he gets home from work."

"Great!" Peter jumped to his feet. "I'd better go do my homework."

As he ran from the kitchen, her grandmother came into the room. "My, who lit a fire under that young man?"

"Granny, I'm so afraid he's going to be disappointed."

"Why, child?"

"He wants Craig to take him fishing on his birthday."

"Oh." Granny sank into the chair that Peter had occupied.

"I told him we'll call him tonight and see if he can. I shouldn't have. What if—"

"Rebecca, have faith. Everything will work out for the best. You just wait and see." Her grandmother patted her hand, then pushed to her feet. "Now, if I don't get moving, we won't have dinner tonight."

"Let me check on Josh and then I'll be back down to help. I think my little man has finally decided to catch up on all the sleep he missed this past week."

Rebecca climbed the stairs to the second floor. She peered at Peter's bedroom door and noticed that it was open. Lately he always closed it when he was in his room. She started to look in, to see if everything was all right with her eldest son, when she heard his voice coming from her bedroom.

She paused in the doorway. Peter had Josh on the bed, changing his diaper and making funny faces at him.

"Okay, big guy, that ought to fix ya right up. Tonight we'll practice extra hard on our walking. Don't want to slack on the job. I want ya chasing me around this house before the year is out. Think of all the things I can teach ya to do." Peter lifted Josh high in the air, then swung him from side to side.

Josh's giggles blended with his older brother's laughter. The sound pierced Rebecca's heart. She cleared her throat.

Peter whirled, surprise evident in his expression. "I heard Josh and thought I'd better check up on him."

How could she tell Peter his dream wouldn't come true for his little brother? The pain in her heart expanded. "Will you watch Josh while I help Granny with dinner?"

"I guess," Peter said, replacing the surprise on his face with his usual sullen expression. But he held his little brother close as though protecting Josh from the world.

Crossing her legs, Rebecca smoothed her black calf-length skirt. Her heart pounding against her chest, she clasped her hands tightly in her lap.

"Chief Stone will see you now," a short, gray-haired woman announced when she appeared in the reception area of the police station.

Rebecca rose, took a deep, calming breath and entered the office the older woman indicated with a wave.

Gabriel came around his desk, offering his hand for Rebecca to shake. "I'm glad you applied. Since the pay isn't much, I wasn't sure you would."

"How could I refuse? Your offer is the only one I've had."

He grinned. "I have to admit there aren't many jobs in Oakview, but we aren't too far from Tulsa where I'm sure you can find a better-paying job."

Warmth flowed through her at his smile, warmth meant to put her at ease, and it did. Her tension evaporated as she responded to his compassion. "I can't spend anymore time away from Josh than is necessary. Driving to and from Tulsa would add an extra hour and half to my work day as well as eat into my salary."

"Who's going to take care of Josh?"

"Granny, until I can come up with a more permanent solution. Peter will help when school is out in a few months and Ann, next door, has volunteered to help Granny until then."

"Josh is welcome here if you get in a bind."

"Then I have the job?"

"Yes. I wish it were more."

"It's a job, and as you know, I need one."

Gabriel sat on the corner of his desk, his stance casual, openly friendly. "When can you start?"

Rebecca noticed him absently twirling his wedding ring on his finger and marveled at the depth of love he must have had for his wife. What would it be like to have a man love her that much? "Tomorrow if you need me," she finally answered after clearing her throat.

"Jenny hasn't been gone more than a day, but her work is already stacking up. If you can start tomorrow, that'll be great." Gabriel rose and headed for his office door. "How's Peter today?"

"Limping around. He hasn't done that much exercise lately, and his muscles are protesting."

"I'm sorry. I didn't realize he was so out of shape."

Rebecca recalled her eldest groaning as he descended the stairs that morning for school. "Don't be. This will be good for him. I don't think he was too upset by the sore muscles. I didn't hear a word of complaint from him at the breakfast table this morning, and he took his tennis shoes to school today. Believe me, lately he's the first to complain if he's upset about something."

"Good. I know it wasn't comfortable for him running around the baseball field in loafers, but everyone who shows up participates. I didn't want him to be any different."

Gabriel brushed against her as he reached to open the door at the same time she did. Rebecca stepped away, nonplussed by the casual touch. Their gazes linked for a few seconds before Gabriel swung the door open and called, "Mabel, I believe you've already met Rebecca Michaels. She's our new file clerk. Rebecca will be starting tomorrow at eight. You'll be working closely with Mabel, helping her with her job."

"Welcome aboard." Mabel pumped Rebecca's hand several times.

"She used to be in the Navy," Gabriel whispered so loud everyone within a few feet could hear.

"And proud of it. I run a tight ship." The older woman's hair was pulled back in a severe bun, her clothes crisp and clean and her stance ramrod straight as though a board were stuck down her back.

"It's nice to meet you, Mabel." Rebecca resisted the urge to rub her arm after its vigorous workout. Even though she hadn't had a job since high school, she knew it was important for her to start out on the right foot with a co-worker. "I'll see you tomorrow."

"Eight sharp."

Rebecca smiled, but she was worried. She knew the value of being on time to a job, especially a new one, but with two children, plans and schedules didn't always work out as she wished. She would just have to get up earlier tomorrow morning. She was determined that Gabriel's faith in her would pay off.

"Mom!" Peter yelled from the top of the stairs. "I can't find my tennis shoes. I have to have them!"

Rebecca hurried out of the kitchen, carrying Josh in her arms. "Where did you put them last?"

"If I knew that, I would know where they were."

She stopped at the bottom of the steps and tried to think where Peter would have put his shoes. Nothing came to mind except the fact she only had twenty minutes to get to work. She was not going to be late the first day. "Okay, retrace your steps yesterday when you came home from practice."

"Mom, I've already done that. I can't remember. I was so tired—" Peter's face lit up, and he spun on his heel and raced for his room. A minute later he reappeared, wearing his tennis shoes. "I kicked them under the bed."

"Why?"

"I was angry at Coach Stone."

"Why?"

"Just was."

Her son's expression closed, and Rebecca knew she wouldn't get an explanation from him. That left Gabriel. She intended to ask him when she got to work *on time*.

Rebecca hurried into the kitchen to finish feeding Josh his breakfast. She propped her youngest in his high chair and started to spoon some cereal into his mouth.

"Here, let me do that, Rebecca. You still have to get ready for work."

Rebecca looked at her grandmother, then at the clock on the wall. She had fifteen minutes to get to work.

Rushing into the small bathroom under the stairs, she ran a comb through her hair and then raced out. Only seven minutes to get to work. She hoped all the police were at the station, because she found herself pressing her foot on the accelerator more than she should. She could imagine the headline in the local newspaper—Newest Member of Police Staff Caught Speeding.

She brought the car to a shrieking halt in a parking space right in front of the building, happy some things were going her way. Hurrying inside, she glanced at her watch and was glad to see she was only two minutes late. She had made it on time—well, practically on time—for her first day of work.

"You're late, Mrs. Michaels. Try to be here on time in the future. There's a lot of work that needs to be done." Mabel stood behind her desk outside Gabriel's office, her expression stern, her stance reminding Rebecca of a drill sergeant.

Rebecca stopped halfway across the room, aware of Gabriel to the side, talking with one of his officers. He turned toward her, a scowl on his face, and her heart sank.

A smile transformed Gabriel's face almost immediately. He said a few more words to the officer, then headed toward Rebecca, his eyes warm with a welcome. "I wanted to be here to greet you your first day at work."

Everything would be all right, Rebecca thought, forgetting other people were nearby while she basked in the warmth of Gabriel's greeting.

He slid a glance toward Mabel, who stood behind her desk watching them, and lowered his voice. "She's tough on the outside but soft on the inside. Give her time."

Rebecca eased her tense muscles and returned Gabriel's smile. "I didn't think I should get a speeding ticket my first day on the job. Probably wouldn't look very good." She peered at Mabel, who was tapping a pencil against her desktop. "But then, maybe I should have."

"Just between you and me, no one's out patrolling at the moment so you'd have been safe. In fact, trying to catch speeders isn't a high priority for this department. But I don't condone that kind of behavior, so don't let anyone know," Gabriel said in a tough voice while merriment danced in his eyes.

"Wild horses couldn't drag it out of me." Rebecca pressed her lips together to emphasize her point, caught up in Gabriel's playfulness. He had a way of wiping away her worries, of making her see this job was a start to a new part of her life.

"Now don't be alarmed, but Mabel is heading this way with a look of determination on her face. I realize her nickname is Dragon Lady, but I don't know what I would do without her. She's been here so long that she knows where the skeletons are buried."

Rebecca turned toward the Dragon Lady, who came to a halt right behind Rebecca. Smile, she told herself, and forced her mouth to curve upward, drawing comfort from the fact that Gabriel was next to her. He made her feel she was capable of doing anything. He made her want to lean on him when she knew she couldn't.

Rebecca stuck her hand out to Mabel. "I'm so glad to be here—"

"Mrs. Michaels," Mabel said, ignoring Rebecca's outstretched hand, "we have a lot of work to do today. With Jenny gone these past few days, things have been piling up. If you're through chitchatting, come with me."

"Yes, Mrs...." Rebecca realized she didn't know Mabel's last name, and somehow she was sure the woman wouldn't want her to call her by her first name.

"*Ms.* Preston." Mabel pivoted and marched toward a desk in the far corner.

Rebecca threw Gabriel a helpless glance, then followed Mabel, all the while eyeing her new desk, which faced a wall with old brown paneling. A pile of folders threatened to topple. Papers scattered across the battered desktop mocked any sense of order.

The older woman waved her hand toward the papers. "I don't like to talk ill of anyone who isn't here, but as you can see, Jenny didn't work much these past few months, ever since she started dating her new husband. I won't tolerate that from you."

Dating or not working? Rebecca wanted to ask, but diplomatically kept her mouth shut. "How long did Jenny work here?"

"Not long, and frankly, even if she hadn't left for Oklahoma City, she wouldn't have been here much longer." Mabel gestured toward the pile of folders. "These cases haven't been filed in a month. This wouldn't have happened if Gabriel hadn't made me take a vacation. I don't tolerate slackers on the job. It's just you and me keeping this place running. And a police department must have order and efficiency to work properly."

Rebecca wondered what the woman did tolerate, but kept her mouth shut. She needed this job, and even though Gabriel was the police chief she suspected Mabel ran things around the station. "I'll do my best."

"You better, or…"

The unfinished sentence hung in the air between Rebecca and Mabel. Rebecca swallowed past the sudden constriction in her throat.

"Now." Mabel placed her hand on top of one stack of folders. "The first thing you need to do is log these into the computer under complaints, then file them over there." She pointed across the large room to a bank of file cabinets. "When you're through with that job, I'll explain what else you need to do."

After Mabel gave her the password to get into the computer files, she strode away. Rebecca released a slow breath while she scanned the messy desk, so out of place in the orderly station. She heard a cough behind her and looked to see Mabel waiting for her to get busy. Rebecca scrambled into the hardback chair and switched on the computer, hoping she knew the software program. She didn't want to ask Mabel for help. She only had so much bravery for one day. Thankfully the computer was similar to the one she'd had in Dallas.

As she checked the hard drive, trying to find a place to log in cases, she couldn't help feeling like a fish out of water. She looked up from the computer and stared at the brown paneled wall in front of her. It must have been part of the station since the sixties. Noticing at least a dozen nail holes in the paneling, she thought about bringing some pictures to hang and maybe some flowers from home to brighten her work area.

"Mrs. Michaels, is there a problem?"

Wincing, Rebecca clicked on an icon and found what she was looking for. "No, Ms. Preston. I've got everything under control."

Two hours later Rebecca regretted saying she had anything under control. She frowned at the offending computer screen, wondering what Mabel would do if she threw it at the brown paneled wall.

"It can't be that bad." Gabriel leaned against the desk, gripping its edge, while he stared at her.

The minute Rebecca saw his face crinkled in a grin, a sparkle in his eyes, the past few hours' troubles vanished. She relaxed in her chair.

"What's wrong? You've been staring at that computer for the past hour as though you're gonna do bodily harm to it. I have to remind you, ma'am, we're in a police station, and that kind of behavior is frowned upon."

"Did anyone bother to check how competent Jenny was with the computer?" she asked with a laugh. "Nothing's where it should be. I've spent the past hour moving files from one folder to another. I haven't had a chance to log in any of these yet." Rebecca trailed her hand up the foot-high stack taunting her. "And to make matters worse, Ms. Preston has been coming over here every fifteen minutes and watching what I do over my shoulder. I can feel her breathing down my neck. I'm sure I have scorch marks on my flesh."

Gabriel's grin widened. "Mabel's just trying to

make sure another Jenny doesn't happen.'' He bent forward, invading her personal space. ''You see, Jenny is the mayor's daughter, and we sort of had to hire her. But I don't think Mabel has forgiven me for that yet. Everything will work out.''

His clean pine scent washed over her, and Rebecca imagined a spring day spent hiking in the woods. ''Easy for you to say. I don't see her dogging your every step. I'm even afraid to take a bathroom break. By the way, where is it?''

''Come on.'' He grasped her hand and pulled her to her feet. ''You haven't had a tour of the station yet, and every new employee deserves at least that.''

With his touch, again Rebecca visualized walking in a pine forest, the sun streaming through the trees, bathing her face in radiance much as his smile did. *Everything will work out.* In that moment she believed those words.

Chapter Five

"This is the jail where we harbor hardened criminals," Gabriel said, touching the small of Rebecca's back as he guided her toward a door. A tingling awareness of his nearness flooded her senses. Her throat tightened, and her pulse sped.

Rebecca noticed all the cells were empty. "Often?"

"On the weekend it picks up. A few people who can't hold their liquor. Occasionally there's a fight. If we're lucky that's all. I'm proud to say there hasn't been a serious crime in Oakview in a year."

"How many police officers do you have?"

"Twelve besides myself. Today you should meet some of them. When you get settled in, Mabel will show you how to dispatch messages to the patrolmen out on the beat." He led her into the main room and pointed toward his office. "That's mine, but you already know that."

Rebecca's gaze fixed on Mabel's desk, which

stood guard outside Gabriel's office. "Who gave her the nickname Dragon Lady?"

Gabriel chuckled. "A man who wanted to see me, and she kept telling him that I was busy."

"Did he get to see you?"

"No. He had to come back later. Mabel has her pluses."

"You didn't want to see him?"

"He was a salesman, and he had a hard time understanding the word no. Mabel helped the poor guy with its meaning."

Gabriel gestured toward another door. "That leads to the rest rooms and the courthouse. Now you've been on the grand tour such as it is. Any questions?"

"When's lunch?"

"Don't let Mabel hear you ask that question on your first day."

Rebecca ignored the twinkle in his eye and said, "I have to let Granny know when I'm going to be home for lunch. She'll need to keep Josh up so I can do his physical therapy with him after I eat."

"Mabel goes to lunch at noon, so you can go before or after her, whichever works best for you."

"I'll try one today, and see if that works best for Granny and Josh."

"Just let Mabel know—"

A commotion at the front door caused Gabriel to turn. He sighed and strode toward an officer, a small, elderly woman and a young man with a beet-red face who appeared as though he would have a stroke at any moment.

"Ben, what can I do for you?" Gabriel asked, eyeing the cuffs on Bess Anderson. "I think, Officer Morris, we can remove those. I doubt Bess is a flight risk."

"She's a menace to society." Rebecca recognized the man speaking as Ben Cross, the owner of a clothing store. "She took a bottle of perfume this time." Anger was in the young man's face as well as his voice. He stepped forward until he stood only a foot from Gabriel. "I demand that something be done this time. You promised you would take care of her."

Gabriel plowed his hand through his hair and drew in several deep breaths. "Now, calm down, Ben. Why don't you come into my office and we'll talk about this?"

"No!" Ben stiffened, his hands balled at his sides. "I want satisfaction this time."

A picture of the young man dueling at dawn popped into Rebecca's mind, and she clamped her lips together. When she couldn't contain her grin any longer, she covered her mouth with her hand.

"Mabel fixes a great cup of coffee. Come on into my office and have a cup while we talk this over."

"No! I can't have this—" Ben floundered for a word to describe Bess "—woman in my store. If people hear I let her get away with this, I'll be robbed blind."

Gabriel rubbed the back of his neck. "Then by all means fill out a report on Bess Anderson. I wouldn't want anyone taking advantage of you."

Ben glared at Gabriel. "Are you making fun of me?"

"I wouldn't do that. A crime has been committed, and you have a right to report it."

Rebecca observed Bess standing next to the officer who had brought her in. She whispered something to the young policeman, then brushed a piece of lint off his navy blue shirt. Next she pulled out a handkerchief and began to polish the officer's badge, all while Ben demanded justice in a loud voice.

"Where's the paper I need to fill out?"

"Come into my office, and I'll fill it out for you."

"What are you going to do about her?" Ben jerked his thumb at Bess, who continued to rub the policeman's badge.

"My staff will make sure she's processed."

While Ben stalked into the office, Gabriel hung back and said, "Make sure Bess is comfortable, Officer Morris. She can sit at Rebecca's desk." Gabriel gave Rebecca a look that spoke volumes. This was not a part of the job he enjoyed. "Rebecca, please get Bess something to drink until I can have a word with her."

When the door to Gabriel's office closed, Officer Morris motioned for Bess to follow him. "Ma'am, you need to have a seat over here."

"Where will you be, young man?"

"I need to fill out a report on this incident."

"You're going to leave me alone?"

Rebecca moved forward. "No, I'll keep you company. Chief Stone wanted me to get you something to drink. What would you like?"

"Tea, with honey and lemon, if you have it." Bess sat in Rebecca's chair, placed her black pocketbook on her lap, then straightened her white gloves and gripped her purse handle.

"Now if I can only find where to get the tea," Rebecca mumbled and plodded to Mabel's desk. "Excuse me. I hate to bother you, but where can I get—"

"Through that door next to the women's rest room is a kitchen. There should be hot water and some tea bags. I don't know about the other stuff. Most of the people around here drink coffee, black." Mabel pulled open a drawer in the bottom of her desk and rummaged through her purse until she produced a packet of honey. "Use this."

"No lemon slices in that purse?"

Mabel almost smiled. "Afraid not."

"Thanks." Rebecca made her way to the kitchen, amazed that the Dragon Lady had a heart, after all.

Five minutes later Rebecca entered the police station with a cup of tea minus a lemon slice but sweetened with honey. As she crossed the room, she heard Ben's raised voice followed by Gabriel's soothing one and cringed. Evidently Gabriel was having a hard time calming the man down.

"Oh, my, that young man is really angry at someone." Bess took the cup Rebecca handed her.

"He says you took some perfume from his store," Rebecca said, pulling up a chair next to Bess in hopes of being able to get some work done while the older woman was at her desk.

"Oh, my, why would he say that? I'd never steal a thing from anyone. Goes against my beliefs."

Rebecca peered at the high pile of folders that still

needed to be logged in, shrugged and replied, "Perhaps you didn't realize it."

"Not realize I stole something? Oh, my."

The hair on the nape of Rebecca's neck tingled. She peered at Mabel. The Dragon Lady shot her an exasperated glare. Rebecca sent her a look that silently asked Mabel what was she to do, toss Bess out of her chair? Rebecca glanced away before she received her answer.

"Maybe you forgot you had it." Rebecca concentrated her full attention on Bess, determined to ignore the look she was receiving from Mabel. Rebecca chose to remember the packet of honey Mabel had given her. That gave Rebecca hope that just maybe she and Mabel could get along.

"I so like to shop, and the home won't let me go to town."

"They won't?"

"No." Bess sipped her tea, her pinkie finger sticking up in the air, her posture prim and proper.

"I wish we had a lemon."

"Why, my dear?"

"Because you asked for it. All we had was honey."

"This is fine. You should come to the home and have afternoon tea with me sometime."

"I would love to. May I bring my grandmother?"

Bess smiled, took another sip of tea and said, "That would be nice." Then she leaned close to Rebecca and whispered, "I don't hear any more shouting coming from that office. Do you suppose the young man has calmed down?"

"I hope so. If anyone can calm him, it'll be Gabriel."

"That man with the nice smile?"

"Yes," Rebecca answered, remembering Gabriel's smile and deciding that was the nicest thing about him. When he directed one toward her, her insides melted and her stomach fluttered.

"People shouldn't waste their energy getting mad. It's so much nicer if people got along with each other. Don't you think so?"

"Yes." Rebecca turned toward Mabel and blew out a relieved breath. The woman was busy working at her desk, her attention on the computer screen in front of her.

"We sometimes have to work extra hard to win some people over, but it's worth it in the long run. I need to bake that young man a chocolate cake, then maybe he won't be so angry."

Rebecca chuckled. "Chocolate works wonders on me."

"Then I'll bake you one, too. How about Sunday afternoon?"

"You don't have to bake me a cake on Sunday."

"No, to come to tea, since you work during the week."

"I'll have to check with Granny, but that sounds fine to me."

"Good. I love to have company. Since moving to the home, I haven't had many people stop by."

Rebecca heard the loneliness in Bess's voice and vowed she would be at tea on Sunday afternoon if she had to bring the whole family, which might not be a bad idea.

The sound of Gabriel's office door opening brought Rebecca to her feet. She chewed on her bottom lip and tried to relax, but in a short time she'd started to care what happened to Bess. She didn't want to see the woman locked up like a common criminal.

Gabriel shook Ben's hand. "I appreciate the compromise."

"Just make sure it doesn't happen a third time, Chief. I'm only doing this because we're friends."

"I understand."

As Ben left the station, Rebecca waited next to Bess, her hand on the back of the woman's chair. Gabriel spoke to Officer Morris. The young policeman nodded, then tore up the paper he had been writing on. Finally Gabriel traversed the room and came to a halt in front of Bess, a neutral expression on his face. Rebecca rested her hand on the woman's shoulder.

"Ben will drop the charges if you'll agree not to go into his store ever again."

"But he has such pretty things."

"Bess, I promised him you wouldn't. In fact, I don't think you should do any shopping for a while."

"I like to shop."

"What if she had a companion with her when she went shopping?" Rebecca squeezed Bess's shoulder.

Gabriel snared Rebecca with his sharp gaze. "Who?"

"Me. I could work something out with the nursing home to take Bess shopping once a week."

Gabriel took Rebecca by the elbow and pulled her to the side. "Are you sure, with all you have going in your life?"

Rebecca tingled where his hand touched her. His scent of pine wrapped her in a cocoon of contentment. "Yes, very. Bess needs someone now. What happened to her? Where's her family?" she asked, forcing herself to concentrate on Bess's problem, not her reaction to Gabriel Stone.

"I don't know. I need to take Bess to the nursing home. Come with me, and we'll talk with Susan Wilson, the director."

Rebecca lifted an eyebrow and glanced over Gabriel's shoulder at Mabel. "Are you sure?"

He chuckled. "Contrary to popular opinion I still do have final say around here." He asked Bess, "Are you ready for me to take you back to the nursing home?"

Bess finished the last of her tea and set the cup on the desk among the mess. "It looks like you could use some help here. I could stay if you needed me to."

"Thanks for the offer, Bess, but I think we have everything under control."

Mabel snorted and mumbled, "That's debatable."

"Come, ladies." Gabriel helped Bess from the chair, then guided her toward the front door. "Mabel, we'll be gone for about half an hour."

"Sure, boss."

"I do believe that was sarcasm coming from Mabel,'' Rebecca said when the door closed behind them.

Gabriel's laugh filled the spring air. "I do believe you're right."

Rebecca slid into the back of the squad car while Bess rode up front. On the short drive to the nursing home, Rebecca listened to Gabriel chat with the older woman with affection in his voice. He had a way with Bess that touched Rebecca. The people in his town were more than just names to Gabriel. Being the police chief was more than just a job to him. He cared about the townspeople, and they knew it.

"You know what I miss the most since I moved to Shady Oaks?" Bess asked Gabriel when he pulled up to the nursing home.

"Your garden?"

"No. I hate getting my hands dirty. I miss my dogs. I had three of them. My niece gave them away when she brought me to the home."

"Why?" Rebecca asked, sliding from the car and opening the door to assist Bess.

"Because dogs aren't allowed in nursing homes. You know, child, animals love you unconditionally. That's the best feeling. Nothing like it. Well, maybe, if you're lucky enough to have the love of a good man." Bess looked right at Gabriel then at Rebecca. "If you know what I mean?"

Rebecca blushed and averted her gaze from Gabriel. She felt him look at her and wished Bess hadn't said anything. They were friends. That was all she wanted, all she could handle right now.

As they entered the nursing home, Rebecca saw

several elderly people in the lounge area off the foyer. One, in a wheelchair, watched a big screen television. Two ladies played a card game in the corner. Bouquets of flowers brightened the area, and their scent pushed the antiseptic odors permeating the building into the background. The place felt homey, Rebecca thought.

Susan greeted them in the foyer, her head shaking, displeasure on her face. "I'm sorry, Gabriel. She got away from us again. Bess, they're playing bingo in the main lounge. Why don't you join the others?"

"Oh, bingo. Next to shopping that's my favorite thing to do." She ambled toward the lounge.

"Don't forget about Sunday afternoon. I'll be here around two," Rebecca called.

Bess paused at the entrance into the game room. "Sunday afternoon? What's happening Sunday afternoon?"

Rebecca blinked, at a loss for words. "I'm coming to visit you."

"Oh, that. Good." Bess disappeared inside the room.

"May we have a few words with you, Susan," Gabriel said, "in your office?"

The director indicated a door on the other side of the large foyer. "Did she shoplift again?"

"Again?" Rebecca asked, following the two into Susan's office.

"Ben caught her taking a watch last week."

"No wonder the man was so upset."

"Have a seat." Susan pointed to two wing chairs

while she sat behind her desk. "I think we've figured out how she's escaping."

Rebecca frowned. "You make it sound like she's in a prison."

"A lot of the people staying here would wander off and not know where they were if we didn't lock the doors to keep them inside. Many of our residents have problems with their memories." Susan turned to Gabriel. "I've fixed the door in the kitchen. It shouldn't happen again."

"I hope not. Ben forgave her this time. I don't know if I can talk him into a third time."

"She didn't remember taking the perfume. I don't think she did it on purpose," Rebecca interjected, thinking how close in age Bess and her grandmother were.

"I agree with you, Rebecca, and that's why Ben finally calmed down. Ben isn't an ogre, but he does have a family to support and lately there has been some shoplifting going on at his store. I think it's kids. He's extra sensitive about it at the moment."

"May I make a suggestion?" Rebecca asked, straightening in her chair as though she were ready-ing to do battle. If need be, she would. "I'd like to take Bess shopping with me once a week. I'll keep a close eye on her and make sure nothing's taken that isn't paid for. She needs someone to care about her. What happened with her family? Her niece?"

"Her niece moved to New York City," Michael said. "That's why she placed Bess in Shady Oaks. With Bess's memory problems, she didn't think the big city would be a good place for her aunt."

"I'll have a word with her niece, but I doubt she'll object to you taking her out for an afternoon. This might help Bess. She seems so lost right now. Her niece had to give her dogs away. I want to give her something to look forward to."

"I have an idea, Susan. My dog had puppies last month. I'll be looking for homes soon for them. I'd like to give Bess one of the puppies to take care of."

"A dog? Here?"

"It's not unheard of to have pets in nursing homes. It would be wonderful therapy for Bess, for all your residents. Bess summed it up when she said animals love unconditionally. That's the best feeling in the world, Susan. If memory serves me, you've got a dog and a cat."

"But if I let Bess have a dog, the others will want a pet."

"Maybe that isn't such a bad idea. Think it over. I'll see if I can get you some literature on it. I'll hold a puppy for a while until you make up your mind."

"I don't know, Gabriel. I can't imagine it staying inside all day."

"You have a fenced yard out back. All I'm asking is that you think about it."

Susan rose. "Fine. Send over any information you have on it, and I'll see. I'll talk with the doctor and nurses and get their opinion."

"That's all I ask." Gabriel opened the door for Rebecca. Outside Shady Oaks he took a deep breath and released it slowly. "Susan does a good job with what she has, but still I wish there was another way to take care of our old people."

"The puppy for Bess was a great idea. I hope Susan approves it." At the squad car Rebecca caught Gabriel's gaze over the roof. "Have you given any of your puppies away yet?"

"The kid next door wants one. Why?"

"I wonder if I could buy one for Peter for his birthday next Saturday."

"No, you can't."

Rebecca climbed into the car, trying to keep the disappointment from showing on her face. "Then do you know where I can get a puppy for Peter?"

"Yes." He smiled. "I won't sell you a puppy, but I'll give you one."

"You will?" Relief flowed through her.

"Lady isn't any fancy breed, but she's a good dog. She wandered into my life not long after Judy died. Just appeared on my porch one morning, cold and shivering. I think the Lord sent her to me to help me mend. She was starving and near death. I nursed her back to life and in the process found a reason to go on."

Tears lodged in Rebecca's throat. Had the Lord sent her Gabriel to help her heal?

"I'm home," Rebecca called as she walked into the kitchen from the garage.

Rose cradled Josh in her lap while she fed him.

Rebecca rushed to take Josh from her grandmother. "I'm sorry I'm late, but I was bound and determined to get all the folders logged on the computer and filed away."

Rose waved her away. "I can handle this. You

know I raised three children. Sit and relax. You've been working all day.''

Rebecca arched a brow. "And you haven't?"

"Taking care of Josh isn't work. It's God's gift to me. He keeps me young.''

Rebecca sank into a chair next to her grandmother and stroked Josh's arm. His cooing eased her weariness. Her children were the reason she was working so hard. They were worth it.

"Where's Peter?" Rebecca asked as she tickled Josh's stomach and relished the sound of his laughter.

"He's still at baseball practice, but he should—" The sound of the front door slamming interrupted Rose. "It looks like he's home."

"Or we have a very loud burglar."

"My gosh, child, work at the police station one day and you're already thinking the worst of the good citizens of Oakview.''

Peter entered the kitchen and headed for the refrigerator. "I'm starved. When's dinner?"

"Six." Rose placed Josh over her shoulder and patted his back.

"How was practice today?" Rebecca asked, watching her eldest son pour a large glass of orange juice and nearly down it in one swallow, then refill it.

He shrugged. "The usual."

"Which means?"

"The team practices catching and batting." Peter rummaged through the cabinets until he found a box of crackers.

"I don't want you to eat too—"

"Mom, I could eat everything in this kitchen and still be hungry. Don't worry. I'll eat dinner. Have you called Dad yet?"

"No, I just got home myself."

"Well, then, what are we waiting for?" Peter took the phone and punched in his dad's number.

While Peter talked with his father for a few minutes, Rebecca steeled herself. She remembered the devastation she had experienced when she had discovered the note Craig left, saying he couldn't take any more and he had to leave—for good.

"Mom! Mom!"

Rebecca blinked and focused on Peter, who was holding out the phone for her. Her hands shook as she took it. "Hello, Craig."

"Peter said you had something you needed to talk to me about. I don't have much time. What is it?"

Rebecca heard the impatience in Craig's voice, and the sound of people's voices in the background. She wondered what their call had interrupted. "Peter and I were hoping you could come up for his birthday next Saturday. He wants you to go fishing with him like you two used to." A long pause on the other end sent her heart pounding against her chest. "Craig?"

"I'm thinking." Another long pause, then he said, "Okay. I can come for a while. I'll be there at seven in the morning. We can spend a few hours together before I have to get back to Dallas."

"Peter will be glad to hear that," Rebecca replied in the most cheerful voice she could muster, while inside she wanted to yell at Craig. *Don't put yourself out for your own son. After all, his feelings aren't as important as yours. He doesn't need to see his own father.*

"I'll have to leave by noon."

"Fine. We'll see you at seven then." She hung up the phone.

"Dad's coming?"

Rebecca nodded, her throat clogged with emotions she couldn't express in front of her son. She laced her hands together to keep them from trembling.

"This is gonna be great." Peter snatched up the box of crackers and the glass of orange juice and left the kitchen.

"Everything isn't as great as Peter thinks?" Rose asked.

Rebecca took her son from her grandmother, needing to hold him close. Burying her face against his hair, she breathed deeply, relishing his baby scent. "No. There were other people at his place, and I could tell he wasn't too pleased by our call."

"Have faith in the Lord, child. Everything will work out."

Rebecca remembered Gabriel saying those same words to her earlier that day. She wanted to believe them. "Granny, I'm trying." She tightened her hold on Josh, drawing strength from her youngest who had been through so much in his short life.

"You haven't told me about your first day on the job," Rose said as she opened the refrigerator to remove some sliced chicken.

"Interesting and challenging."

"Challenging?"

"Not the actual work so much as how to get along with my co-worker." Rebecca started to tell her grandmother about Mabel when the doorbell rang. "I'll get this then tell you."

She swung the front door open and found Gabriel in cutoffs and a sweatshirt. He filled the entrance with his overwhelming presence. She greeted him with a smile, pleased to see him. Her spirits lifted.

"What brings you by?"

"I wasn't there when you left today, and I wanted to know how the rest of your first day on the job went." His gaze trekked down her.

"Checking for scorch marks from the Dragon Lady?"

He chuckled. "Are there any?"

"One or two. Come in."

"I'd better stay out here. I'm in desperate need of a shower after running laps with the team."

"How's Peter doing? Giving you any trouble?" Rebecca came out onto the porch.

"No, he hasn't complained since that first day. Actually he ran next to David today. For the first lap they carried on a conversation."

"Good, because this morning I was concerned something happened at practice yesterday."

"Why?"

"He came home and kicked his tennis shoes under the bed."

Gabriel chuckled. "Probably because he's done more work these past couple of days than he's done in a month's time." He raked his fingers through his sweaty hair. "I have to give him credit. He's done everything the team has done." Leaning against the railing, he folded his arms across his chest. "Okay. How was your day?"

She sat in the swing and turned Josh in her lap so he could see Gabriel. "The job's fine. I'll win Mabel over. I think she was shocked that I wasn't out the door right at four-thirty. I think I further shocked her by staying until all the files were logged and put away."

"I bet you did. When I first came to work as the police chief, I had to win Mabel over, too. Just because I was the boss meant nothing to the woman."

"Since you're still the police chief, there's hope for me."

"There's always hope, Rebecca. I think that's one of the messages the Lord was giving us when He sent us His only son."

Fear nibbled at her. Dare she have hope? Rebecca thought about Peter's birthday. She prayed that Gabriel was right.

Chapter Six

The crack of the bat against the ball echoed through the park. Rebecca leaped to her feet and yelled as David Carson headed for first base, then pushed on to second. A runner came in to home plate, and everyone in the dugout rushed to greet him with high fives and cheers.

Rebecca found Peter among his teammates, huddled around the boy who had come in for the tying run. A huge grin was plastered on her son's face. Seeing Peter with the others, excited and part of the team, gave her hope that soon he would come to accept their move and maybe even grow to like living in Oakview.

With that thought, Rebecca searched the crowd filing into the dugout for Gabriel, the one partially responsible for this change in her eldest son. When she spotted him bending over and speaking low to the next batter, she smiled at the intense expression on Gabriel's face. He didn't take this game lightly. He was an all-or-nothing kind of guy. He had taken Peter under his wing and was determined to make her son part of this town. Her heart warmed at the thought.

She relaxed and drew in a deep, calming breath. The scent of recently mowed grass permeated the air. Spring was definitely here, she thought, shedding her sweater. She lifted her face to the sun and savored its warmth.

The next batter came to the plate and swung two times to no avail. The third pitch flew past the ten-year-old, low and outside. The ump shouted, ''Ball.''

''I think I have bitten off every fingernail I have,'' the woman next to Rebecca said.

Rebecca tilted her head to look at the young mother sitting on her left. ''Is that your son at bat?''

''No, David is my son. He's on second.''

''Then you're Mrs. Carson.''

''Please, call me Alicia.''

''I'm Rebecca Michaels. My son is the team manager.'' She pointed toward Peter, who was placing bats in holders while his gaze was fixed on the batter.

''David has mentioned Peter. They worked at the church a few Saturdays back with Gabriel. My husband said they accomplished quite a bit. We always appreciate any help we can get. Keeping a church up outside is as much work as inside.''

Rebecca wasn't going to mention what had led her son to ''volunteer'' to clean up the church that Saturday. ''I know what you mean. The same applies to a house. But then the church is the Lord's house.''

''That it is.''

The sound of the bat hitting the ball riveted Rebecca's attention to the scene in front of her. The ball sailed toward right field. A member of the other team positioned himself under it and readied himself to catch it. If he caught it, they would go into extra innings. She held her breath.

The boy fumbled the ball. It plopped to the ground and rolled toward the fence. He scrambled for it while David headed for third. The boy in the outfield retrieved the ball and threw toward the pitcher. David rounded third for home plate. The pitcher lobbed the ball toward the catcher as David slid in for the winning run.

"Safe," the ump called.

Rebecca released her pent-up breath, jumped to her feet and shouted, "Way to go. You did it!"

Alicia threw her arms around Rebecca and hugged her. Joy transformed Alicia's plain face into a radiant one. Rebecca pulled away, beaming with her own bright smile.

"David was so worried about this game. The Hornets were the best team in the league last year. This is a big victory." Alicia lowered her voice. "And if the truth be known, Samuel, my husband, told me that Gabriel stayed up most of last night worrying about this game."

"Men and their games," Rebecca muttered and searched for the man in question.

Gabriel stood in the midst of his team, receiving congratulations from the boys and giving them his. Then he quickly had the team form a line to greet the Hornets on the field. He turned to make sure everyone was in front of him. He saw Peter putting equipment away. He walked over to her son and said something. Peter appeared surprised but followed Gabriel to the end of the line, then planted himself in front of Gabriel as everyone walked onto the field.

Rebecca's heart ached as she watched her son being included in the celebration, giving high fives to all the Hornets who filed past him. Tears crowded her eyes, and she quickly blinked to rid herself of them before someone saw her.

"David says your son is a fast runner. We're one man short. Has he considered going out for the team?"

Alicia's question drew Rebecca's attention. "Gabriel's working on Peter."

"Then it shouldn't be long before he's playing with the Cougars. Gabriel can do just about anything he sets his heart to. And he has such a way with kids. Too bad he doesn't have children of his own. He and Judy were so much in love. If only Judy—"

"Mom, did you see me?" David ran to his mother, smiling from ear to ear.

Rebecca thought about Alicia's comments. She agreed that Gabriel would make the perfect father. Why couldn't Craig be more like Gabriel? Peter and Josh deserved a father who loved them and accepted them as they were. And, Rebecca thought, I deserve a man who loves me and—

Hold it, Rebecca Michaels! What are you thinking? She had no right even to contemplate a relationship with Gabriel. She didn't want to become involved with any man outside friendship, and she certainly didn't have the emotional strength to fight a ghost for a man's love. Gabriel was still deeply in love with his deceased wife, or he wouldn't be wearing his wedding ring.

"Are you and Peter going to come to Pizza To Go with the rest of the team?" David asked.

Rebecca concentrated on what the child was asking her instead of on the man walking toward her. "I don't know. Peter hasn't said anything." Out of the corner of her eye, she saw Gabriel come to a stop a few feet from her. Her heartbeat quickened.

"You've got to. Everyone goes after a game."

Gabriel greeted Alicia with a smile, then said, "I insist on Peter and you coming to Pizza To Go. It's an unwritten rule that every team member must be a part of the celebration afterward."

"Peter can but I'm not a team member," Rebecca said with a neutral expression, desperately trying to keep her pulse from racing so fast that she became dizzy. That was what she deserved for even considering Gabriel as a potential—a potential what? Oh, my, as Bess would say. Rebecca felt heat suffuse her cheeks and wished she was anywhere but where she was.

"I could always make you an honorary team member, if that's what it takes to get you to the pizza place."

She brought her hand up. "Stop right there. I can't hit a thing and I certainly don't run fast. And worse, if I saw a ball coming toward me, I'd run the other way. You wouldn't want me on your team."

"But you're already part of my team." His eyes gleamed.

Her heart hammered a mad tempo against her chest. "I am?"

"You work at the police station, don't you?"

"Yes," she answered, mesmerized by the warmth dancing in his eyes, all directed at her. Oh, my.

"Then I rest my case. You're a member of my team."

Alicia laughed. "Rebecca, give up. You won't win this argument. Once you're a friend of Gabriel's, you're a friend for life."

"That you are."

His grin reached out to Rebecca and enveloped her in a sheath of empathy. Yes, they were friends, Rebecca acknowledged, but that would be all and she had to remember that.

"Well, put that way, I guess Peter and I will be there."

"It's out on the highway."

"Yes, I know. Peter has already conned me into going there once."

"What kid doesn't like pizza? Come on, let's get everyone moving toward the parking lot. I've worked up quite an appetite."

"Gabriel Stone, you always say that." Alicia tousled her son's hair. "Right, David?"

"Yep, Mom. Coach, I don't think it'll take much to get us moving."

Gabriel chuckled. "David, I don't think it will, either." He cupped his hands to his mouth and announced in a loud voice, "Time to celebrate. We have a party to go to."

Everyone on the team cheered, then scrambled to

get their belongings and hurry to cars with parents following more sedately.

Alicia walked with Rebecca. "I'll see you at the pizza place."

"I have to first swing by and get my grandmother and my youngest son."

"Then let me take Peter with me and David."

Peter came to Rebecca's side at the car. "That's okay, Mrs. Carson. I need to help Mom with Josh."

Rebecca gave her eldest son a perplexed look but said, "We'll be there soon." She climbed into her car and waited for Peter to slide in on the passenger's side. "I can get Josh and Granny by myself, hon, if you want to go with David."

"Mom, I know you don't care that much for pizza, so if you want to stay home, that's okay by me."

"Since when are you passing up a pizza? What's going on here, Peter?"

"It's not my victory. I'm just the team manager. I didn't do anything, so I don't feel like celebrating." Peter hunched by the window, drawing in on himself. He averted his face and stared at the passing landscape.

"Hon, you can always play. Chief Stone would love to see you do that. But you're wrong about not being a member of the team. You're an important part."

"I'm not hungry."

Rebecca didn't have to see her son to know his bottom lip was sticking out. "We promised Chief Stone we would be there."

"You just want to see him. He's always at our house. You work for him now."

"Is that what this is about? Do you think I have romantic feelings for Chief Stone? He and I are friends, Peter. That is all." If she said it enough, she might begin to believe it. On Gabriel's part, that statement was true. On her part she wasn't sure anymore. He jumbled her feelings all up into a tight knot that was solidly lodged in her stomach.

"Yeah, sure, whatever."

"Hon, I think we should talk about this. I work at the police station because that was the only job available right now. I was lucky to get work in Oakview."

"Mom, I said I'll go. Don't make a big deal out of it."

"But you said—"

"Forget what I said. Coach Stone is okay by me."

Rebecca pulled into her grandmother's driveway, turned the engine off and faced Peter. "I love you, honey. You never have to worry about that. No one will ever come between us."

Peter bit his lower lip, his eyes shiny. "I know, Mom."

Gabriel saw a couple entering the pizza place and frowned. Where was she? Rebecca had said she was coming. Alicia had told him she was going to stop by and pick up Rose and Josh. She should have been here by now. Gabriel glanced at his watch for the tenth time in the past twenty minutes. His worry grew. What if she had been in a wreck? What if—

"She'll be here soon," Alicia said from across the

table. She winked at her husband, who had joined them a few minutes ago. "Isn't that right, Samuel? Traffic can be beastly at this time of night."

"Yeah, seven o'clock on a Friday night in Oakview we often have traffic jams. You should know that, being the police chief and all."

"Funny, you two," Gabriel said over the noise of thirteen boys all waiting for their pizzas to be made. "I'm just concerned that something might be wrong. She works for me. I think I have a right to be concerned."

Alicia barely contained her smug smile and the twinkle lightening her eyes. "Of course, Gabriel, you have a right since she is your employee."

Gabriel scanned the crowded restaurant. Half the patrons were team members and their families. The players sat at two tables close together, and every boy was talking at the same time. The noise level didn't bother him. The cramped chairs pushed together so everyone could sit in a group didn't bother him. But not knowing if Rebecca was all right bothered him—a lot.

When had he started to care so much?

The minute she had opened the door the first day he had met her. He'd looked into her big blue eyes so full of sadness and he'd longed to erase that look from them. He was always a sucker for someone who needed comfort. Ever since Judy had died he felt it was his mission to help others through their pain. That was the only reason he was so concerned about Rebecca, he told himself, twisting his wedding ring.

"Ah, she's here," Alicia announced and scooted

her chair around so there would be room for Rebecca, Rose and Josh.

David called Peter to his table and made room for him while the waitress delivered four large pizzas to the boys. Gabriel stood as Rebecca and Rose approached him. Gabriel pulled a chair out for Rebecca, while Samuel did the same for Rose. When they were seated, the reverend whistled to get the boys' attention. They all bowed their heads. Gabriel slanted a look at Rebecca, who held Josh against her.

"Lord, bless this food we are about to partake and thank you for the win this evening." Samuel sat again, laughing. "I hope He can forgive me for saying such a short prayer. I didn't know how much longer the boys would have waited."

"It was to the point." Rose placed her napkin in her lap. "Here, Rebecca, let me hold Josh while you get settled."

"That's okay, Granny. I have everything under control."

Gabriel suspected Rebecca had forgotten how to ask for help. He knew Rebecca's husband had done little to assist her with Josh and Peter. Was that why Rebecca insisted she had everything under control when Gabriel felt that she was being pulled in different directions?

"I haven't gotten to see this little tiger in a few days. Come here, Josh." Gabriel didn't give Rebecca a choice. He reached out, took her youngest from her and swung him high. Josh's giggles were music to his ears. His smile and bright eyes were a balm to Gabriel's soul. When he settled Josh in the crook of his arm, he felt content, complete, as though something missing in his life was found. Was he letting his feeling toward Josh and Peter influence his growing feelings toward Rebecca?

Gabriel chanced a look toward Rebecca and wasn't surprised when he saw her mouth slightly open, her eyes round as saucers. "I'm a take-charge kind of guy. Sorry." He shrugged but didn't give Josh back to her.

He knew she felt she should hold Josh, take care of him throughout the meal, perhaps not eat, so she could see to Josh's needs. Gabriel was determined not to let her hide behind her son.

She opened her mouth to say something. Gabriel stuck a piece of pizza into it. "Isn't that delicious? They make the best, I believe, in the state of Oklahoma."

She mumbled something around the food and sent him a glare that told him he didn't want to know what she had said.

"I'm glad you agree with me. I'll let Harry know how much you like his pizza." Gabriel sent her an innocent look and cuddled Josh closer.

While Rebecca finished the large bite she had been fed, Gabriel played with Josh, giving him a bread stick to hold. Her son grabbed at the new plaything and gripped it for a few seconds before dropping it.

Rebecca saw the exchange between Gabriel and Josh. She scanned the faces at the table to gauge their reaction to the fact her son had a hard time holding onto objects. Alicia smiled at her. Samuel was busy talking with Rebecca's grandmother.

"You have the most adorable son. How old he is?"

"He'll be two in a month." Rebecca waited for the reaction that usually followed that announcement.

"Oh, great. I love planning a birthday party. I hope you'll let me help."

"You'll have to stand in line, Alicia. I have first dibs." Gabriel took a bite of his pizza, still cradling Josh.

"Here. Let me hold him so you can eat." Rebecca wiped her hands so she could take Josh.

"You get to hold him all the time. You've got to learn to share, Rebecca. He's happy right where he is. Enjoy your dinner."

"I could always call the police chief of this town and put in a complaint that you've kidnapped my son. I've got connections. I work for him, you know."

"I like to live dangerously. Want me to dial the station for you?"

Rebecca laughed. "No. It would be hard to hold a baby, eat and dial a phone all at the same time. Something would have to give."

"Have you all noticed how quiet it is?" Alicia asked, glancing at the tables full of Cougars.

"Thankfully, they are practicing good manners and not talking with their mouths full. There's hope after all." The reverend finished his pizza and patted his stomach. "Delicious. If I wasn't watching my weight, I would finish that last piece on the platter."

"That's okay. I'll take the temptation away so you

won't suffer." Gabriel reached for the last slice and plopped it on his plate.

"A true friend," Samuel said with a chuckle.

"My duty as a policeman is to protect you, even from yourself." Gabriel lifted the pizza to his mouth. "I take my job seriously." He bit into the slice and chewed slowly.

As the boys finished eating their food, the noise level in the restaurant skyrocketed. Rebecca ate her portion, having to agree that the meal was good even though she wasn't a big fan of pizza. Suddenly the room grew quiet. Rebecca looked up and saw the waitress bringing out a big cake with ten candles lit on it.

Gabriel started singing the happy birthday song, and all the boys followed. When they got to the name, they shouted Peter's, and Rebecca thought she would cry. Tears welled into her tight throat as she watched her eldest son struggle to keep his emotions under control. He was speechless when the woman placed the huge cake with his name on it in front of him. He looked at Rebecca with a question in his eyes. She shook her head and shrugged.

"Guess it's time to give you Josh back," Gabriel said, and transferred her youngest to her arms.

Gabriel rose before she could question him about the cake.

"Peter, when the team found out it was your birthday tomorrow, they wanted to show you their appreciation for joining us with this little celebration. The fact we won tonight makes this party even sweeter." Gabriel moved to the counter and retrieved a package. "This is for you from us." He handed Peter a large, long gift, wrapped in blue paper with a baseball motif on it.

Stunned, Peter took the gift and held it.

"Open it!" The chant filled the restaurant.

Peter tore into the package. When he lifted the leather baseball glove and bat for everyone to see, Rebecca wiped the tears coursing down her cheeks with the back of her hand. Her grandmother gave her a handkerchief that smelled of roses, Granny's special fragrance.

"Isn't that sweet," Rose whispered to Rebecca. "I bet Gabriel was behind this."

Rebecca knew he was. He was determined to show her son he was a part of the team.

"Speech!" The new chant came from the thirteen boys sitting around Peter.

Peter opened his mouth then clamped it closed, a stunned expression on his face.

"I think he's speechless," David said.

Peter mumbled his thanks while cradling his two gifts to his chest.

Gabriel sat again. Rebecca reached over and took his hand, squeezing it. "Thank you." She couldn't say another word. A huge lump in her throat prevented her from speaking.

He laid his hand over hers. "Anytime. A lot has happened to him this past year. I just wanted him to know he was special to us."

"Well, I don't know about everyone else, but I want a piece of that cake. If I know Gabriel, it's chocolate on the inside and from the bakery at the supermarket. They bake the best cakes in town. To die for.'' Alicia moved to the boys' table to take charge of cutting the cake and handing out slices.

"I'm afraid the cake I baked is gonna look puny next to that monster." Rebecca reluctantly withdrew her hand from Gabriel and immediately felt bereaved.

"Yours doesn't have to feed a score of people. I do have to admit I went overboard when I ordered it. There may be some leftovers."

"Some? Try half." Rose took the piece passed to her and started eating.

"That's our police chief. He never does anything halfway," the reverend said, and popped a forkful of cake into his mouth. "Mmm. This frosting is wonderful. Melts in your mouth." He ran his tongue over his upper lip. "Remember the time you chased those robbers into the next county?"

"I got my men."

"Yeah, but you nearly caused a wreck out on the highway."

Gabriel paled. "Oh, please don't remind me of that folly. Occasionally I see red when someone takes what isn't theirs."

"One of your pet peeves." The reverend ate another bite.

"I'm trying to practice restraint. It just doesn't always work."

"We all have our faults. The Lord didn't make us perfect." Samuel paused, then said, "Speaking of not being perfect, George is getting out of prison soon."

Gabriel stiffened, all color gone from his face. His hand shook as he placed his fork beside his plate. "I know."

"You have to forgive him sometime, Gabriel."

"No, I don't." Gabriel rose. The sound of his chair scraping across the wooden floor permeated the silence that hung at the table of adults. "If you'll excuse me—" He pivoted and left the restaurant.

"Who's George?" Rebecca asked, aware of the strain at the table.

"The man who drove the car that killed Gabriel's wife and son. He was drunk." Samuel Carson looked at the door Gabriel had disappeared through. "I should go talk to him. This wasn't the right time to bring that subject up, but I thought being among friends would lessen the pain."

Alicia patted her husband's hand. "Let Gabriel have some time alone before you approach him."

Rebecca's heart broke. She wanted to go to Gabriel and ease his pain, as he had hers these past few weeks. But she didn't have a right to, and she realized she wished she did.

Gabriel drove his fist into the punching bag hanging on his back porch. Again and again he hit the imagined face of the man who had robbed him of his future. Sweat poured off him, clinging to his T-shirt and shorts, but still he worked out his anger and frustration until exhaustion made it impossible for him to lift his arms.

He sank to the porch floor, rid himself of his gloves, then buried his face in his hands. He could still see the wrecked car with Judy inside. She had died on the way to the hospital. The doctors had done an emergency C-section to try to save his son, born two months too early.

George McCall was responsible. Gabriel wished he could rid himself of his hatred toward the man as easily as he had his boxing gloves. He couldn't, and he felt as though he had let God down. He had tried. The anger was still embedded deep in his heart, and he wanted the man to remain behind bars. Judy and their unborn child had been Gabriel's life. He went through the motions of living, but he knew something had died in him that day along with his wife and son.

"Our Father, who art in heaven, hallowed be thy Name. Thy kingdom come. Thy will be done, on earth as it is in heaven. Give us this day our daily bread. And forgive us our trespasses, as we forgive those who trespass against us. And lead us not into temptation, but deliver us from evil. Amen." Gabriel murmured the Lord's Prayer. It should be a guide to him in his forgiveness of the man who had killed his wife and child. "Please, dear Lord, give me the strength to do what I must."

"Mom! It's after seven," Peter called from the living room.

Rebecca cleaned Josh's face after more of his breakfast ended up on him than in him. She placed him in his swing and went into the living room. "It's only fifteen minutes after seven. Your dad lives several hours away. He's just late. Relax, Peter. Watch some TV until he comes.''

Peter gave her a look that said she must be crazy, which might be true. She didn't like him to watch much television, and here she was encouraging him to.

"I don't want to miss him when he pulls up." Peter turned to the window and stared out.

Rebecca saw her son's new fishing gear—a gift from Craig—stacked in the corner by the front door. She noticed he had on his lucky fishing jacket. Worry nibbled at her composure. If Craig didn't come, she didn't know what she was going to do.

When she walked into the kitchen to clean up the breakfast dishes, she glanced at the clock over the stove. Craig had often been late. She hoped this was one of those times.

But twenty minutes later, she resolved to call him. At least that would end her son's ordeal.

Quietly she lifted the receiver and punched in Craig's number. On the third ring he picked it up, and Rebecca's grip tightened on the phone until her knuckles were white.

"You haven't even left yet?" she asked, instead of saying hello to his greeting.

"Sorry. I overslept."

Rebecca heard no remorse in his voice. She inhaled a deep, fortifying breath, then blew it out through pursed lips. "Are you coming?"

"Nah. Too late. I have to be back this afternoon. I have plans."

"Plans that are more important than being with your son on his birthday?"

"Tell Peter I'll call him later. Did he get my present?"

"Yes. He has all his gear packed in the new tackle box and it's by the front door while he waits at the window for you. Please talk to him."

Craig mumbled something under his breath, then said, "Put him on."

Rebecca went to the door to the living room and said, "Your dad wants to talk to you."

Peter frowned. "Is he on his cell phone? Did his car break down?"

To spare her son's feelings, for a second she thought about lying. "No, he's at home."

"But—" Peter hung his head and shuffled into the kitchen to pick up the phone.

Rebecca listened to her son's one-word replies, watching his shoulders sag. She put her arms around him and held him against her while he mumbled goodbye to his father. Peter dropped the receiver, missing the cradle. She tightened her arms about him. When a beeping sound blared, Rebecca put the phone where it belonged.

"He's not coming. He doesn't know when he can see me," Peter finally said, his body shaking.

Rebecca kissed the top of his head. "He'll come as soon as he can. We'll have a great day, anyway."

Peter wrenched himself from her embrace. His face turned red, and his eyes narrowed. "My birthday is ruined! I don't want to do anything!"

He raced from the room, and Rebecca heard him

run up the stairs and slam his bedroom door. She sucked in deep gulps of air, trying to calm the thundering beat of her heart. *Lord, why are You doing this to my family? Peter is an innocent. He doesn't deserve this from his father.*

When the sound of Josh's swing stopped, she started toward it to take Josh out but halted halfway across the room. Her youngest son had grasped the bar and stalled its movement. He held his grip for a good twenty seconds before letting go, the swing falling backward.

Tears flowed down Rebecca's face. In the midst of Peter's disaster, Josh had done something he never had before. Even though tears streamed down her cheeks, she smiled and picked up her youngest son. Maybe God hadn't deserted her family, after all.

"Where did you learn that, my man?" she asked, surprised by the strength he'd shown. She hugged Josh to her, listening to his cooing, relishing his baby scent.

She held him in front of her, staring into his sweet face. "Your big brother isn't happy. What do you think we should do?"

Josh made some more sounds, his eyes bright.

The puppy! She would ask Gabriel to bring it over early. Maybe that would take Peter's mind off his father.

With Josh in her arms Rebecca placed a call to Gabriel, realizing as she listened to his line ring that she hadn't seen him since he walked away from the restaurant the night before. She started to hang up when his gruff voice said, "Hello."

"Gabriel, is this a bad time?"

"Rebecca? No, I was just working out. A little out of breath. What's up?"

"Peter's dad backed out of coming today. Is there any chance you could bring the puppy over this morning?"

"You bet. I'll shower and be right over."

As she put the receiver in its cradle, Rebecca wondered what Gabriel needed. When she had last seen him, he had been devastated by the news of George's release. That had been twelve hours before. He was always coming to her aid. Today she was determined to come to his and help him. If he would let her.

Chapter Seven

"Rose let me in," Gabriel said as he entered the kitchen and placed a cardboard box on the floor.

"Thanks for bringing the puppy. I know it's early. I probably interrupted you, but—" The words died in Rebecca's tight throat. She swallowed, but the dry ache deep inside her threatened her fragile composure.

"Don't you worry about interrupting me. That's what friends are for. To be there when others need them." He studied her from across the expanse of the kitchen.

She saw the evidence of his sleepless night in his face and suddenly wanted to comfort him. "Gabriel, about last night at the pizza place."

"Forget last night. This is about you. About Peter."

The gruffness in his voice, the pain that briefly flashed in his eyes closed off that topic of conversation. He could comfort, but he didn't want comfort.

A seed of hurt buried itself in her, and she had to shut it down before she was caught up in a different kind of pain.

"Did Craig say anything about why he couldn't come?"

She shook her head. "I don't understand how he can do this to Peter. He's just a little boy." Tears glistened in her eyes, blurring her vision.

He came to her and drew her into his embrace. "I'm sorry, Rebecca."

She had done so well until he touched her and held her close. The comfort of his arms, his soft, soothing words, opened the dam holding her tears. They spilled out unchecked. She cried, soaking his shirt, the faint thump of his heartbeat close to her ear, a rhythmic sound enticing her to find peace. She felt the calming stroke of his hand on her back and couldn't shake the sensation that she had come home, that this man would protect and support her.

When there was nothing left inside her, she pulled back slightly and looked into his face. It was filled with compassion, and there was a touch of sadness in his eyes. She smiled.

"You seem to be coming to my rescue a lot lately." A whimpering sound came from behind Gabriel. Rebecca peered around him and saw the white and brown puppy trying to get out of the carton.

"What do you think? Will Peter like her?"

"She's beautiful." Rebecca disengaged herself from Gabriel's arms and knelt next to the box, scratching behind one of the puppy's ears, which flopped over.

"Beautiful? More like a funny mix of several breeds that weren't meant to go together. But if she's anything like Lady, she'll be perfect as a boy's pet."

"It's all in the eye of the beholder." She lifted the puppy out of the box and held her up. The whimpering stopped. Big brown eyes stared at Rebecca, and she was lost. She hugged the warm, cuddly animal, finding its scent as appealing as a baby's. "If she doesn't help Peter forget his troubles, I don't think anything will."

"Where is he?"

"Upstairs in his bedroom."

Gabriel swept his arm out. "Lead the way. We have some cheering up to do."

Cradling the puppy in her arms, Rebecca walked through the living room, checking to make sure Josh was asleep in the swing. As she climbed the stairs to the second story, she sensed Gabriel's gaze on her, and a blush flamed her cheeks. She remembered the feel of his arms about her, and the blush deepened. A warm, tingling sensation left goose bumps all over her body. If she wasn't careful, she would come to depend on him too much.

She knocked on her son's door, waited for him to say come in, and when he didn't, she eased it open a crack. "Peter? Someone's here to see you."

Peter leaped off his bed. "Dad?"

Her smile died. "No, honey, you know he won't be able to come. Chief Stone is here with something to show you."

"I don't wanna see anyone." He plopped down on the bed and turned his back to her.

She opened the door wide and entered. "He brought you a gift."

"I'm not—" The puppy made a noise, and Peter twisted around to look. His eyes widened, but he stayed on the bed, almost as though he were afraid to move for fear the puppy would vanish. "Whose dog is that?"

"When Chief Stone heard you always wanted a pet, he thought you might like one of Lady's puppies." Rebecca approached the bed and sat, extending the animal toward Peter. "That is, unless you don't want her."

Something snapped in her son's eyes. He swung his legs around and sat up, taking the puppy into his arms and burying his face against her small body. "She's mine?"

"She's yours if you promise to take care of her," Gabriel said, coming into the room. "I don't give just anybody one of Lady's litter."

Peter looked at him, a serious expression on his face. "Oh, I'll take great care of her. I promise." A beaming smile split his face as he focused his attention on the puppy wiggling in his arms.

"What are you gonna name her?" Gabriel asked.

"I don't know. I have to think on that," Peter answered as though it was a grave matter. The puppy licked his finger, then began to gnaw on it.

"It took me a week to decide on Lady's name."

"It did?" Peter got on the floor with his new pet and let her waddle around.

"Hon, she isn't housebroken."

"She won't do anything, Mom."

The puppy proceeded to urinate on the throw rug. Rebecca watched Peter wince as he snatched his pet in midstream and got wet.

"Ugh! Mom!" Peter threw her a beseeching glance.

"I'll go get something to clean up both of you."

Rebecca left the room. Gabriel knelt on the floor next to Peter, who held the puppy at arm's length. "You know animals, like people, don't always do what we want."

"Yeah, I see."

"They can disappoint us." Gabriel removed a handkerchief from his pocket and gave it to Peter.

The child wiped his arm and hand. "Tell me about it."

"Do you want to talk about your dad not being able to make it this morning?"

Peter frowned. "No, there's nothing to talk about. My dad was too busy to come see me. It happens." Shrugging, he brought his pet to his chest and stroked her.

"Yeah, it happens, but that doesn't mean it doesn't hurt us when it does."

"I'm okay. It was just a dumb old fishing trip. I didn't want to go that bad, anyway."

"That's a shame. I was hoping you wanted to go fishing. I know a great place we could all go. We could take a picnic lunch, do some fishing and go hiking in the woods. There are several nature trails we could take."

Peter continued to pet his puppy, but his movements slowed as though he was thinking on what Gabriel had said.

"Of course, this is my own special place. You'll have to swear to keep it a secret. I don't want too many people knowing about it, or all the good fish will be gone."

Peter slanted a look at Gabriel. "Where?"

"I have to show you."

"Can Josh and Mom come, too?"

"Yeah, sure, even Rose."

Peter tilted his head and thought for a long moment. "Can I bring my puppy?"

"I don't see why not. If she's like Lady, she'll love the outdoors."

Peter scrambled to his feet. "Then let's go. Before it gets too late."

Gabriel laughed. "How about this?" He gestured toward the wet spot on the throw rug.

"Oh." Peter grinned as Rebecca came into the room, carrying a spray bottle, paper towels and a sponge. "Mom will take care of it."

Rebecca thrust the cleanup items into her son's hands while taking his pet. "No, Mom will not. You might as well learn now how to do it."

"But we—"

"No buts, Peter Michaels. If your dog messes, you clean up."

Peter knelt and placed a paper towel over the puddle, muttering something about not having the time.

While her son worked on the mess, Rebecca looked toward Gabriel. "What's going on?"

"We're taking his birthday party to a little spot I

know. How quickly can you prepare a picnic lunch and get ready to enjoy yourself outdoors, fishing, hiking and whatever else we fancy?''

"Where?'' Rebecca asked, never one to go blindly anywhere without details.

"Mom, it's a secret. Coach won't say. He has to show us his special place,'' Peter said, spraying the spot on the rug with half the bottle's contents.

"Hon, I think that's enough.'' Rebecca took the cleaning liquid from Peter.

"We need to get moving. I want to show Mrs. Wiggles the outdoors. I know she's gonna love going on hikes with me.''

Rebecca held a squirming Mrs. Wiggles for Peter to take. "It might be a while before she can go on long walks. I don't think her legs will take her very far.''

"I'll be her legs until she can follow me.'' Peter slapped on his ball cap and started out the door.

Rebecca stared after her son. "What happened here?''

"I made an offer he couldn't refuse?''

Rebecca folded her arms and quirked one brow.

"Okay. People love other people's secrets, and I told Peter I would show him where my secret place was.''

"How secret?''

"Oh, probably only about half the county knows.''

"Only half? So how many others are going to be joining us at this *secret* place?''

"No one, at least I hope not. It's on a piece of property I own outside of town.''

"I didn't know you owned land in the country."

"There's a lot you don't know about me, Rebecca Michaels."

"Aren't you the man of mystery?"

"There's a lot I don't know about you, too."

"True."

"But that's the fun of new friends. Getting to know them." Gabriel walked past her and out the bedroom door.

She followed, watching the casual way he moved, not a wasted motion. *Friends.* That's what they were. Nothing else, Rebecca thought, trying to ignore the bittersweet pang piercing her heart.

Rebecca used her body to shut the door on Gabriel's four-wheel drive, then lugged the two bags of food they had brought on to the plaid blanket spread on the ground. She set the food beside a cooler that was filled with soda and ice. Surveying all they had brought, she had to laugh. Josh sat propped in his swing so he could see his surroundings. Granny sat in her lounge chair, and Gabriel and Josh headed for the stream with their tackle boxes and fishing poles.

Rebecca adjusted the awning on Josh's swing. "I think we have half our house here," she said, sitting in the chair between her youngest and Granny.

Her grandmother patted the arm of her lounger. "All the comforts of home. That's the way I like to commune with nature."

The sound of the stream flowing over rocks and the birds in the nearby trees soothed Rebecca, and she closed her eyes and let the sun bathe her face.

She inhaled a deep breath, the scent of the woods behind her filling her nostrils with pine and earth, a potent reminder of the man responsible for them being here.

Gabriel had given her son a reason to celebrate on his birthday. Peter's laughter filled her with joy. "This is heavenly."

"That it is, child. God knew what He was doing when He created this spot."

Mrs. Wiggles yelped. Rebecca opened her eyes to find the puppy trying to escape the leash that confined her movements. Her son's new pet saw him on the bank, casting his line, and wanted to be with him. "Getting Peter a dog was the best thing I've done in a long time." She rose and untied Mrs. Wiggles, who scampered after Peter.

"I can think of a few more things you've done that were just as good."

"What?"

"Becoming friends with Gabriel. Letting him help you. Child, you don't let people help you often."

"Why, Granny, that's not true. I came to live with you."

"But you insist on doing everything. I have to practically arm wrestle you to hold Josh, to feed him."

"I don't want to be a burden to anyone, especially you, after you were so gracious in opening your home to me and my children. Besides, you're taking care of Josh while I work—at least until I can come up with a more permanent solution."

"You're family. Family is meant to rely on each other. Don't you know that?"

Rebecca found her floppy white hat and put it on. "I suppose I do in here—" she touched her head "—but not in here." She laid a hand over her heart.

"You've closed your heart."

"I can't afford to be hurt again like Craig hurt me. I can't let my family be hurt like that. It's safer not to depend on anyone but myself."

Again Peter's laughter drew Rebecca's attention. She looked at her son reeling in his line, and knew he laughed because of the man next to him. She owed Gabriel a lot. She wished she didn't owe anyone a thing. Owing meant ties, and ties meant emotional involvement, which could leave her open to being hurt again.

Peter held up a small fish for her to see. "The first one, Mom. But we're gonna throw it back because Coach says it's too small to eat. You only keep fish that you'll eat."

"Then you'd better get busy. I'm mighty hungry for fish."

"You don't like fish."

"Well, any fish you catch, I'll eat."

"Promise?"

"Yes."

Peter cast his line into the water, then sat on the bank next to Gabriel, listening to something he was saying. Her son's head was bent toward Gabriel, and she could tell what Gabriel was saying held her son's interest.

"You know, Granny, Gabriel may be good at

helping others with their problems, but has anyone helped him through his?''

''What problem?''

''His wife's untimely death.''

''Gabriel has dealt with that.''

''Has he? Remember last night when Reverend Carson mentioned George McCall was getting out of prison? Gabriel went pale and excused himself. He didn't come back. That isn't the action of a man who has completely dealt with his wife and child's deaths.''

''I see what you mean. Maybe you could be there for him. The Lord sends many messengers to do His work.''

''I'm not a messenger for the Lord. My life's in such a shambles. I wouldn't know where to begin to help another when I'm struggling with my own problems.''

''Nonsense, child, you're very capable of helping others. Come to church tomorrow with me, if not for yourself, then for your children.''

''Peter went with you last week. I have to stay home to take care of Josh.''

''It's not what you say but how you act in life that has a lasting impression on children. Josh can stay in the nursery while you go to the service.''

''But—''

''Others can take care of Josh. He's not a burden. He's a delightful child. Just because Craig wouldn't have anything to do with him doesn't mean others won't.''

Gabriel gave Peter his fishing rod and rose. He

walked to Rebecca. "I'd like to show Josh how to
fish."

He hadn't worded it as a question, but he waited
for her to say something before picking up Josh.

"He'll have to wear his hat. I don't want him getting sunburned." Rebecca rummaged in the tote for
Josh's cap, found it and gave it to Gabriel.

"See what I mean?" Granny asked when Gabriel
took Josh to the stream and sat with him in his lap.

Rebecca watched Gabriel place Josh's hands on
the pole then cover them with his larger ones. The
man was constantly doing simple things to make her
care about him. He probably wasn't even aware of
what he was doing. She needed to put some emotional distance between them or she would be lost,
her heart broken for the second time in her life. She
only had to look at Gabriel's ring finger to have that
confirmed.

"You're right, Granny. It isn't fair to my children
to impose my feelings on them. I'll go with you to
church tomorrow, but I'll feel better if I take Josh to
the service. He should be pretty quiet."

"Suit yourself, but our nursery staff is quite capable of taking care of him."

"I'll think about it."

Peter leaped to his feet, letting out a yell. "This
has got to be a big one."

Her son struggled to reel in the fish. Ten minutes
later Rebecca groaned, realizing she would be eating
fish for lunch.

"Look what I caught!" Peter displayed his catch,
his chest thrust out in pride. He marched to a second

cooler filled with ice and put the fish in it. "You're gonna be so lucky. Coach says his pan-fried fish is to die for."

She smiled at her son. "That's what I'm afraid of."

"I want to take Mrs. Wiggles for a walk."

"I don't want you to go far. I know this is Chief Stone's land, but—"

"Oh, Mom, Coach said I would be okay on the trail. Quit babying me. Why don't you fish for a while until I get back? Keep my spot warm."

"Good idea, Rebecca. And I'll take Josh and feed him his snack. I think he's probably worked up quite an appetite fishing."

Rebecca arched an eyebrow. "Granny, you can stop right there," she said while Peter scooped up Mrs. Wiggles and started for the path that led into the woods. "I know what you're up to."

"More fish. That one in the cooler is for you. There are three more of us that would like some fish for lunch."

"I'll gladly share mine."

"No need for that. Go get us some more."

Her grandmother smiled too sweetly as she followed Rebecca to the stream and took Josh from Gabriel.

"I think Josh was getting the hang of fishing. I had to let go for a second, and he still held onto the pole." Gabriel watched Rebecca sit, his eyes shadowed by the low brim of his baseball cap. "Have you fished before?"

"Once when I was a child." She picked up Peter's

pole and looked at the end of the line. "What do I bait it with?"

"This." Gabriel thrust a wiggling worm at her.

She shrieked.

He chuckled. "Obviously I'll have to do the dirty work."

"If you want me to fish." She wrinkled her nose and eyed him while he slipped the worm on the hook. "I thought fishermen used lures nowadays."

"Peter and I had too much fun digging around for worms."

"So that was what you two were doing in the backyard while I was slaving away getting all the food ready."

Rebecca settled on the rock with Gabriel next to her and her line in the water. She slid a glance toward him. "You haven't done very well so far."

"That's a challenge if I ever heard one. Okay, if I get the next fish, you have to do something I want. If you get it, I'll have to do something you want."

"Nothing against our beliefs? Nothing illegal?"

Gabriel pressed his hand over his heart. "Rebecca Michaels, I'm shocked you would ask. After all, I am the police chief." He winked. "You're just gonna have to trust me."

His chuckles were as warm as the sun caressing her skin, leaving her tingling all over. His familiar male scent of pine again reminded her of the woods behind her. His eyes glittered with a carefree promise. "Okay. I'll trust you. It's a deal."

As he focused on his pole, there was nothing casual about him. He was a man on a mission, and

Rebecca began to have doubts about the wisdom of agreeing to the challenge. She turned her attention to her fishing rod. She needed to win the challenge. That look in his eyes should have alerted her to the danger of agreeing to the dare.

When she got a nibble a few minutes later, she scrambled to her feet, beaming, and began to bring in her line. "I haven't quite decided what I'll have you do, but—"

The line went slack. Rebecca opened her mouth to say something and closed it without speaking. "It's gone," she finally said when she reeled in the line and saw the empty hook.

Gabriel baited it for her. "Easy come. Easy go."

Rebecca sent the line flying through the air, determined to win. Her thumb slipped. When she glanced at the rod, she saw a tangled mess, and realized it would take hours to unravel the snarl she'd made of Peter's line. She pulled the hook in by hand. The best she could hope for was that Gabriel wouldn't catch anything, either. At the moment she would settle for a tie.

She sat on the large boulder they shared, her body only an arm's length away from his. "Well, at least I got a nibble. You've been there all morning and haven't gotten one bite."

"Is that disappointment I hear in your voice? You hadn't even decided what you'd have me do, whereas I know exactly what I want you to do."

"You do?" she murmured, picturing in her mind Gabriel cupping her face and leaning down—

"I've got one."

He rose with the intention of making sure his fish didn't get away. His every move was full of purpose as he reeled in his line. Rebecca's mouth went dry as the minutes to her defeat neared. When Gabriel swung the fish out of the water and onto the bank, beads of sweat popped out on her forehead. Anticipation and dread mingled to form a knot in her stomach.

Gabriel did short work of taking the fish off the hook and putting it in the cooler. Then he turned to her with a predatory gleam in his eyes. He stalked toward her. She took a step back and almost lost her footing.

"Watch it, Rebecca. I know it's spring, but that water is cold."

Rebecca glanced at her grandmother, who was happily feeding Josh and talking to him. No help there.

Gabriel stopped in front of her. "What in the world do you think I want?"

Her voice refused to work. She shook her head.

Laughter glinted in his eyes. "What happened to that trust you said you had?"

She gulped. "It's there—somewhere."

He clasped her upper arm, deliberately prolonging the suspense.

"Enough. What do I need to do?"

The corners of his mouth lifted. "I want you to come with me Wednesday night to choir practice. Rose says you have a great voice. We could use another singer in the church choir."

The picture of them kissing dissolved into disappointment. Rebecca felt the heat of her embarrassment at what she had been thinking. She was sure it had been written all over her face, too.

With laughter still in his eyes, Gabriel leaned close and whispered, "When we do kiss, it won't be on a bet. That you can be sure of."

He released his grip on her arm and pivoted, leaving Rebecca shaken to the core. "What time do you want me there?"

"I'll pick you up at six forty-five," he said without looking back.

Her trembling hands clasped in front of her, she watched him retrieve the two fish from the cooler and begin to fillet them. She pulled herself together and walked the short distance to the bags holding their food. She needed to keep busy. She couldn't believe she had wanted him to kiss her right there in front of everyone. She was setting herself up to be hurt. This evening she would have to have a strong talk with herself about that. She couldn't take much more of this seesawing back and forth with her emotions concerning one Gabriel Stone.

Peter bounded out of the woods, Mrs. Wiggles in his arms. "I saw a baby deer."

"Was its mother nearby?" Gabriel pulled out a frying pan and placed the fillets in it.

"Yeah. They heard Mrs. Wiggles yelp and fled. Can I help build the fire?"

"Sure. We need twigs. Can you gather some?" Gabriel made a fire pit in the sand and put a ring of stones around it.

Peter brought back enough twigs to start a fire.

Gabriel showed him how to lay the twigs properly, then he lit them, blowing on them to get the fire started.

As Gabriel and Peter worked, Rebecca observed them and couldn't shake the feeling Peter's father should be showing him this. When the twigs caught fire, Gabriel set the grill and pan over the flame.

Was Gabriel involved with her and her family because of her or because of her two sons? Were Josh and Peter a substitute for the son he lost? The questions came unbidden into her mind as she stared at the two of them working together. There was something going on between her and Gabriel. But what was it?

Peter watched Gabriel for a few minutes, then headed for the stream with Mrs. Wiggles in his arms. When her eldest son saw his fishing pole, he said, "Mom! It's ruined."

Gabriel glanced up. "Nah. I can fix it later. I was hoping, though, that we could throw the ball some."

Peter's frown evaporated. "Okay. But I'm not very good."

"Is that why you don't want to come out for the team?"

Peter stared at his feet but didn't say anything.

"I can help you with throwing and batting, Peter. We can start this afternoon if you want."

Rebecca held her breath. In Dallas Peter had always been active, playing with his friends. She hated to see him alone.

Peter scuffed the toe of his tennis shoe in the dirt.

"It don't look like I'll be fishing anymore, so I guess so."

Rebecca relaxed her tense muscles and continued arranging food on the blanket. When she lounged on her haunches and eyed the lunch before her, she smiled, pleased at what she had managed to throw together on the spur of the moment. Several bags of chips—corn, potato and tortilla—a fruit salad, rolls, pickles, carrots, celery sticks, a three-way bean salad and a chocolate sheet cake with chocolate icing adorned the blanket.

As the aroma of frying fish mingled with the scents of fresh water and forest, her stomach rumbled. Her son had caught a fish, and Gabriel was cooking it. She couldn't ask for a better way to have one of her least favorite dishes.

"Come and get it," Gabriel announced to the group.

Rose propped Josh in his swing, then set it in motion. Rebecca passed out paper plates, plastic forks and napkins.

After the fish was served and the other food dished up, Gabriel said, "Lord bless this food and watch over the people here today partaking in this wonderful feast. When things seem the toughest is when we need You the most. Give us the strength to see beyond our own lives and to be a messenger for You."

When Rebecca glanced up after the prayer, she found him staring at her with an intense look that took her breath away. She'd felt a sweep of emotions today, from joy to despair. She'd witnessed a small miracle when Josh had grabbed the bar on his swing with enough strength to hold it for twenty seconds. Had she given up on the Lord too soon? Was there some purpose only God knew behind all her family had encountered this past year?

She knew what she would have asked Gabriel if she had won the challenge. She wanted him to trust her with his feelings regarding his wife and George McCall. She wanted him to lean on her for a change.

She observed him laugh at something her grandmother said, then fork a slice of fish into his mouth. By the expression on his face he enjoyed every bit as he chewed then took another bite. His eating reminded her that Gabriel was an all-or-nothing kind of guy. He had given his heart once. Could he give it again?

Chapter Eight

Peter held Lady's last puppy close to his chest as he sat next to Rebecca in the lounge of the nursing home the following afternoon. Bess strolled into the room, surprise brightening her expression when she saw Rebecca, Peter and Gabriel on the couch.

"Oh, my, they told me I had visitors. I had no idea so many." Bess crossed the room. "What have you there, young man?" She stroked the puppy in Peter's grasp.

"A gift for you."

"Oh, my, for me." Bess pointed at herself. "May I hold him?"

"It's a girl." Peter held the puppy up for Bess to take.

"I can't believe she's mine." Bess eased into the chair across from them and brought the puppy to her face, breathing deeply. "I've missed this smell. I don't know what to say." She shook her head. "That's not true. I know exactly what to say. Thank you." She looked from Rebecca to Peter, then finally to Gabriel. "I hope you can stay for tea."

Rebecca swallowed several times before saying, "My grandmother wanted to be here, too, but Josh, my youngest, fell asleep, and she decided to stay home with him. She hated missing meeting you and seeing you get your new pet."

"She's really all mine?" Bess's eyes were large, her hand continuing to stroke the puppy as though reassuring herself the animal was real.

The wonder in Bess's voice gave Rebecca a sense of satisfaction she hadn't felt in a long time.

Gabriel shifted on the couch. "Bess, there are some ground rules I told Susan you would follow concerning your pet."

Bess rubbed her cheek along the puppy's fur. "What?"

"She'll have to stay outside during the day in the garden area. She can sleep in your room at night as long as she doesn't disturb anyone. And Susan wants all the other residents to enjoy her, too."

"But what about bad weather?"

"Peter and I are going to build you a doghouse so she'll be fine during bad weather."

"You're going to do that for me?" Bess stared at Peter.

He nodded, his shoulders thrust back, a pleased look on his face.

Gabriel leaned forward, resting his elbows on his knees and loosely clasping his hands. "Bess, this is for a trial period. If this doesn't work, I'll have to take the puppy back. Susan wasn't sure if this was a good idea, but I know it is.''

''Of course, it is. Peepers and me will do just fine.'' Bess straightened in her chair with the puppy curled in her lap. ''Now, young man, tell me about yourself. Do you have a dog?''

For the next hour Rebecca relaxed and enjoyed herself, sitting between Gabriel and Peter and listening to them talk about the best breeds of dogs. When it was time to leave, everyone had decided that a mutt was the best breed.

On the drive to her grandmother's, Peter inundated Rebecca with questions concerning the nursing home and Bess Anderson. Finally she held up her hand and said, ''Peter, I think you should volunteer at the home. I know you and Gabriel are going to build the doghouse for Peepers, but I bet some of the people would love to have you read to them. Some of them have poor eyesight and can't read anymore.''

Peter leaned forward, a puzzled expression on his face. ''But, Mom, when? I need to work on my batting and throwing and then there's the team practices several times a week.''

''Hon, if you want to do something, you'll find a way. Think about it.''

He relaxed, suddenly quiet. When Gabriel pulled into her grandmother's driveway, Peter scrambled from the Jeep and hurried toward the house.

Rebecca laughed. ''I have a feeling before long he's going to hate leaving Mrs. Wiggles, especially for school.''

"Then there's practice after school," Gabriel said, turning the engine off and twisting so he faced her.

"Such dilemmas for him."

The mellow atmosphere in the car shifted. Rebecca was acutely aware that she was alone with Gabriel—if a person could call being in a car in broad daylight on a fairly busy street alone. His particular scent wafted to her and swirled about her, drawing her into his sphere of influence.

"In the past few days I've seen some of the old Peter coming through. Thank you for your help." Rebecca flattened herself against the passenger side door and rested her left arm along the back of the seat.

"It was nothing."

"Nothing? Gabriel Stone, you have a way with people. You genuinely like them, and they in turn like and respect you—even my son. That is nothing? You're supposed to say you're welcome and accept the praise graciously."

He shrugged and smiled sheepishly. "I suppose that's one of my downfalls. I get uncomfortable when someone says something nice about me." His grin widened. "But you're welcome, Rebecca. I appreciate your kind words."

"See. That wasn't so bad. You didn't choke or anything." She looked at her hand loosely curled in her lap then into his warm gaze. "I would like to return the favor. I want to help you." She was finding the word *want* was too mild for what she was feeling. *Need* was more like it.

"I don't need any help. Everything's fine."

"Is it? For the past two days we have avoided talking about Friday night at the pizza place."

A cloud moved into his eyes—dark, ominous. "There's nothing to talk about. We ate. We went home."

"And we talked about George McCall."

Gabriel stiffened, all casualness gone from his expression. His brows slashed downward. His eyes narrowed. "What do you want me to say? That I'm afraid of what I'll do when I see the man? That my thoughts are anything but Christian?" He gripped the steering wheel, his knuckles ghostly white.

Rebecca waited for a long moment before she answered. "I want you to talk to me. Let me help you through this pain you're feeling. If not me, then at least talk to someone else. It's eating you up inside, this anger you're feeling."

"It's not anger, Rebecca. It's guilt."

"Guilt?"

"Yes. I saw George driving earlier in the day. I didn't pull him over or anything. If I had, my wife and child would be alive. Do you know what that does to a man?" Gabriel yanked open his door and bolted from the Jeep.

Rebecca sat with her mouth slightly open and watched him storm down the street. The anger in his body wasn't directed at George, but at himself. She realized mixed up in that anger was a deep, soul-wrenching pain that was tearing him up inside. She hurriedly climbed out of the vehicle and ran after him.

Rebecca grabbed his arm to halt his escape. "Gabriel Stone, how dare you drop a bomb like that then go stalking off down the street.''

He rounded on her, a war of emotions playing across his face. ''I have nothing else to say. You wanted to know what was going on. Now you know.'' A neutral expression finally settled in place as though nothing of importance had happened a few minutes before.

She released her grip on his arm and stabbed her thumb toward his vehicle. ''And what do I do about your Jeep in my driveway? I may have plans for later today. I don't particularly relish trenching my grandmother's front lawn in order to get my car out.''

He glanced toward the vehicle in question. ''Oh.''

''Oh, is right.''

He strode toward the Jeep. Rebecca hurried to keep up. At the driver's side she threw her body between Gabriel and the door.

''We need to talk about this.''

''Why do women always want to talk?''

''Why do men always want to ignore what they're feeling?''

He glared at her, his arms rigid at his sides. ''Because talking doesn't always help.''

''Then listen,'' Rebecca said, trying to breathe normally. His nearness made her heart beat way too fast. She had no one to blame but herself. She'd placed herself in this position, so close her hands itched to touch him.

He arched a brow. ''Listen?''

''Yeah. Hindsight is always one hundred percent. How could you know what George was going to do later in the day? Was he driving recklessly at the time you saw him?''

His scowl darkened. ''I thought you only wanted me to listen.''

''Was he?''

''No, but I knew about George's drinking problem.''

''The accident wasn't your fault. Period.''

''Easy to say. Hard to believe.''

''I can't make you believe that, but you're beating yourself up over something you had no control over.''

''Kinda like you?''

She pulled herself up straight. ''What do you mean?''

''Did you have any control over your husband leaving you?''

''No.''

''Did you want him to leave?''

''No.''

''Then why are you beating yourself up over something you couldn't control? We can't control everything around us. And hiding from life won't give us any more control over it.''

Gabriel stepped so close she could feel his breath on her face. She sucked in a deep swallow of air that did nothing to relieve the tightness in her chest. She pushed him away and slid from between him and the Jeep. ''You have a way of turning things around. You're good at avoiding discussions about yourself.''

"Boring subject."

"Only to you," she said, without thinking through what she was admitting.

"You think I'm interesting?"

"I didn't say that."

"But you implied it." He grinned. "Admit it, Rebecca Michaels."

She glared at him. "Yes, I think you're interesting."

His grin broadened.

"But then I think all my friends are interesting or they wouldn't be my friends."

"Right. Friends."

She wanted to scream. "What do you want me to say? We *are* friends. I'm not ready for more, and you certainly aren't either."

Leaning against the Jeep, he folded his arms across his chest. "Why do you say that?"

She wasn't sure what drove her to touch him, but she did. She took his left hand and held it in front of his face. "This. A man who wears his wedding ring isn't ready to move on."

He stared at his ring finger then at her, surprise flittering across his face, as though what she had said was news to him. "You're right," he admitted slowly.

"And all of my energy has to be directed at holding my family together and getting back on my feet."

"Then I guess it's friends." He thrust his hand toward her to shake.

She took it in hers and felt a jolt streak up her

arm. "Yes," she declared in a strong voice, while inside she felt as if she were lying to herself—and him.

Wednesday night Rebecca sat in the front pew, listening to the choir sing. Their voices rang loud and clear in the church, filling it with beautiful music. She was glad he won the fishing challenge and wanted her to come to choir practice.

When the song was over, Gabriel said, "We'll take a ten-minute break, then finish practicing for the Sunday service."

He strode to Rebecca. "Well, what do you think? Care to join us?"

She shook her head. "I don't sing for other people anymore."

"Then who do you sing for?"

"Myself. Sometimes Josh."

He eyed her. "Are you shy, Rebecca Michaels? If so, there's nothing to be shy about. You'll be one of many. I promise I won't have you do a solo unless you want to." He held up his hand as though he was swearing in court.

"I don't think—"

Alicia sat next to her on the pew. "Oh, come on, Rebecca. We can always use another voice. Besides, we have the best seats in the house."

"But I'll have Josh with me during the church service."

"I know Rose wouldn't mind taking care of Josh during the service." Alicia patted her hand as though everything was settled, then called to another choir member and hurried over to her.

"Gabriel, I can't ask Granny to take care of Josh on Sunday. She does during the week."

"Then there's the nursery. Mabel is in charge of it, and she does a great job."

"Mabel!" Rebecca could picture the nursery, all the babies lined up as though they were in the military.

"Now, Rebecca, Mabel's wonderful with the children. There's a side of her you haven't seen."

"I think I'll pass."

"All I ask of you is to try it one time. If it doesn't work out, not another word."

"Is that a promise?"

"Yes."

"One time and then you won't say another word?"

"Yes."

She smiled sweetly at him, intending to suffer through one half of a practice and one service. Then that would be it.

Gabriel took her hand and pulled her to her feet. "Come on up and join us. We're gonna practice 'Oh How I Love Jesus.'"

By the time the choir practice was over thirty minutes later, the group had made Rebecca feel welcome. She stood by Alicia, who talked to her between songs and introduced her to everyone. When Gabriel wanted to put Rebecca in the front row, Alicia insisted Rebecca would be better off in the back. He hadn't argued.

"Good night, Rebecca," Alicia said and waved goodbye to her.

Once all the members had left, the sudden quiet in the church seemed disconcerting after all the noise. Rebecca watched as Gabriel turned out the lights. The only illumination that streamed into the sanctuary came from the large door she held open. He approached her. She plastered herself against the paneled door to keep it open. She suddenly realized they were alone. Everyone else had cleared out fast, wanting to get home to their families.

She licked her lips and forgot to breathe as he waited for her to walk out of the church. He fell into step beside her, taking her hand.

"I'm glad you didn't mind walking tonight, Rebecca. I just couldn't pass up such a beautiful night."

She relished the strong feel of his hand holding hers. Staring at the dark sky with stars beginning to glitter in the blackness, she had to agree. "Walking's nice. I wish I had more time to exercise. I used to a lot before—" Her words trailed off.

"Before what?"

"It's not important. I just decided I need to stop thinking about my life in terms of before my divorce and after my divorce."

"Explain."

The softly spoken command mingled with the sound of the insects chirping, compelling her to open up to Gabriel. She felt the comfort of her hand nestled in his. She smelled the scent of a spring night, laced with honeysuckle growing nearby.

"I'm not sure I can."

He stopped in the middle of the sidewalk and drew her in front of him. He took her other hand. "Try, please."

"Before Craig walked out on us, my life revolved around trying to please him, trying to be the perfect wife and mother. I would spend hours keeping the house clean and making sure the meals were just what he wanted. I forgot who I was in the process. After he left, I was forced to discover the person I am. I'm still working on that." She attempted a smile, which wavered. "Being a single parent is hard. It's doubly hard when deep down you're not sure who you are."

"Rebecca, that's where the Lord can help. Turn to Him. Seek answers from Him."

"I'm not sure it's that simple."

He shook his head. "I never said it was simple. Really become a part of the church and you'll see the way."

A car passed, and the driver honked. Rebecca used the distraction to step away from Gabriel. He waved to the driver, then turned his attention on her again.

She wished the moon wasn't so bright. She could read the question in his eyes and didn't have any answers for him. She was still trying to figure out who she was. How could she commit herself to God when she was floundering so much?

"Come on. It's getting late, and I know we both have to be at work early."

"And I can't be late. After being on the job for two weeks, I finally got Mabel to smile at me today.

I almost brought out the confetti but was afraid of her reaction when I started throwing it.''

"See? I told you she was a pussycat," he said with a chuckle and began to walk again.

"More like a tiger."

"Ah, I have faith in you. You'll learn to handle her in no time."

A warmth suffused her at his words. *I have faith in you.* If she could only restore her faith in herself. Maybe then she could believe in the power of God again.

Rebecca held Josh, not wanting to turn him over to Mabel. Maybe she should forget singing in the choir today. Or maybe she could hold Josh while she sang. That shouldn't be too difficult. He only weighed a little over twenty pounds.

"Mrs. Michaels, are you going to leave your son?" Mabel asked, waiting at the door to the church nursery.

"Please call me Rebecca, at least at church," she said, delaying. Her mind frantically came up with one excuse after another not to leave Josh.

"There are other parents behind you." Mabel's voice softened.

Rebecca glanced over her shoulder and offered the two couples behind her a smile. "Sorry. First-time jitters."

She stepped to the side and let the other parents drop off their children. She noticed they had no qualms about giving their babies to Mabel. Rebecca knew that the church would be careful to whom they entrusted their children, but she hadn't left Josh with a stranger—not that Mabel was really a stranger, but to Josh she was.

After the other parents walked away, Rebecca faced Mabel again and thrust Josh at her before she talked herself out of it. Mabel took Josh in her arms, cradling him in such a tender way that Rebecca was speechless. She tried to form words, but she couldn't. She watched the Dragon Lady coo at Josh and grin like any grandmother. The smile that graced Mabel's mouth transformed her face into a countenance Rebecca wouldn't have believed if she hadn't seen it with her own two eyes. The Dragon Lady was a different person when she smiled.

Mabel peered at Rebecca, a softness in her expression. "Do you have his bag?"

Rebecca blinked, breaking the trance. "Yes. Here." She handed the tote to Mabel, who placed it on the floor next to the door.

"Are there any instructions…Rebecca?"

Hearing her name on the woman's lips for the first time surprised Rebecca. Yes, she realized she had asked Mabel to call her by her given name, but she had honestly thought Mabel would ignore the request. "He likes to watch people. He just needs to be propped up with pillows, in case he loses his balance while sitting, or you can put him on a pallet on the floor or in a crib. Whichever works for you. I'll be back immediately after the service."

"You aren't going to the adult class after the service?"

"Yes, but I'll take Josh with me."

"Why? He'll be fine here with me and the other children."

Rebecca wasn't sure how to answer the woman. She had been forced to leave Josh with her grandmother five days a week to go to work. She felt bad enough about that. Josh required so much care, and she hated others having to do it. She never wanted her son to feel she had abandoned him.

Someone touched her on her shoulder. She pivoted to find Gabriel standing behind her. Her heart raced at the sight of him. She smiled.

"Church is going to start soon," he said, returning her smile. "Ready for your debut?"

"You make it sound like I'm going to sing a solo." She slanted him a look. "I'm not, am I?"

"Of course not." He began walking toward the sanctuary. "I'm glad to see you here, dressed in your choir robes. I wasn't sure you would join us."

"I said I would." She thought about her moment of faltering at the nursery door and decided not to tell him how close she had come to backing out.

"Josh will be fine with Mabel."

"I know in my head that I need to share my care of Josh with others. That's a fact that has come home quite a lot lately. It's just hard to convince my heart. I have protected him from the day he was born. He has always known I was there for him no matter what."

Gabriel paused at the door to the sanctuary. "Who have you had to protect him from?"

"Some people find it hard to accept a child with special needs."

"Who?" He looked deep into her eyes. "Your ex-husband?"

Rebecca laid her hand on his arm. "Craig never tried to harm Josh. He just wouldn't have anything to do with him. He completely ignored Josh, as though he didn't exist from the day he was born. It broke my heart to see it."

"I'm sorry, Rebecca. Not all men—people are like that."

"I've just learned to be protective when it comes to Josh. As he gets older and he's more aware of people's reactions to him, it will hurt him."

"He's one of God's children. It won't happen here." He covered her hand and squeezed gently. "Not if I'm around."

Basking in his words, Rebecca connected with Gabriel on a level that startled her, her gaze trapped by the fervent appeal in his. He made her feel special, important. If only that were true, she thought, and slipped her hand from his arm. He had been pulled into her family because of her children. He was drawn to her two sons. She was thankful for that, but she realized she wanted more.

Rebecca followed Gabriel to the front of the church where the choir sang. She passed her grandmother, Peter and Bess, who had come with them. Bess waved at her. Rebecca waved back, responding to the woman's joy at coming to the service with Rebecca's family. Peter whispered something to Bess, and the older woman smiled, patting his leg. Rebecca wished she had thought about inviting Bess to the church, but it had been Peter's idea. Her son felt a bond with the woman. Their pets were sisters, he'd told her this morning.

The service flew by. She started singing her first song, and before she realized it, she sang her last note. Listening to Gabriel's solo performance had moved her beyond words. She had heard some of it in practice Wednesday night, but for some reason after Reverend Carson's stirring sermon on God's forgiveness, Gabriel's tribute had touched something deep inside her. She remembered their conversation earlier in the week about George McCall and wondered if it had struck Gabriel as deeply as her.

As the congregation filed out of the sanctuary, Rebecca hung back. When only a couple of women were left, she sat in the pew and savored the quiet serenity. She felt at peace—as though God had reached down and blessed her. Could it be possible that there was a reason for all that had happened the past few years? That He hadn't forsaken her and her family?

Slowly she rose and walked from the church, reluctant to leave. In the foyer she noticed some people milling about, but most were making their way to their Sunday school classes. She hurried to get Josh.

At the nursery she stopped in the doorway and watched Mabel cuddling her son in the crook of her arm while she read a story to the other children who weren't sleeping. Her animated voice surprised Rebecca. Mabel threw her whole self into the story, making it come alive for the children. Even Josh was listening and looking at Mabel. Quietly Rebecca backed out of the nursery, her assessment of Mabel changing.

"See? Didn't I tell you Mabel was good with the kids?" Gabriel whispered in her ear.

Rebecca sucked in a deep breath. She felt his breath on her neck and shivered. She edged away from the nursery before replying, "You were right. I'll stop worrying about Josh."

"No, you won't, but then mothers are supposed to worry about their children."

"Not just mothers."

The mischievous gleam in Gabriel's eyes dimmed. "No, fathers should, too. And most would."

Rebecca knew there were injustices in this world. Gabriel not being a father was one of them. "You can still be a father, Gabriel. You're a young man," she replied to comfort him, then blushed when she realized what she had said. "I mean—"

He placed his finger over her mouth. "Shh. I know what you mean."

Do you really? she wanted to ask. There was a part of her that fancied rescuing Gabriel and another part that wanted to run as fast as she could away from him and what could be if circumstances were different in their lives. But circumstances weren't different. He was still in love with his deceased wife, and she was scared to commit to another man.

Chapter Nine

A gentle breeze blew as Rebecca stepped onto the patio and breathed deeply of the flower-scented air. She threw her head back and relished the sun's rays on her face. After several days of rain, she welcomed this perfect seventy-degree weather. A perfect Saturday. Staring at the cobalt blue sky, she noticed not one cloud.

The sound of hammering lured her attention to the two guys in her backyard. They had been working diligently for the past few hours. Peter's head was bent over a board, intense concentration on his face. Gabriel studied a sheet of paper, a frown marring his expression. They both wore cutoffs and white T-shirts with tool belts about their waists.

"Ready for a break?" she called.

Her son hit a nail one last time, then stood, the hammer dangling from the tool belt Gabriel had given him at the beginning of the doghouse project.

"Mom! Come look at what Coach and me have done so far."

She made her way toward the pair. Her son looked like a small version of the guy who used to build and remodel homes on the public broadcast station. Gabriel rose, too. He looked like a larger version of the same guy. Like father, like son. The phrase popped into her head, and she stopped short. Were Peter and Josh replacing Gabriel's deceased son? Were her two boys the reason he hung around so much? She shook the disturbing questions from her mind, determined not to let anything disrupt their evening.

"It's starting to look like a doghouse. I see three walls. Is that the roof over there?" She pointed to two pieces of plywood.

"I'm going to ignore that teasing tone and take your words at face value. I never said I was a builder, carpenter or anything remotely in that industry, but Peter and I are two intelligent guys who can surely figure out these blueprints." Gabriel held up the instructions he had purchased from the hardware store.

"I have all the confidence in the world in you two. I fixed some lemonade, and Granny baked some chocolate chip cookies. Peter, you can go get some if you want."

"Oh, great," Peter said, racing toward the back door, the hammer slapping against his side.

"I guess we're ready for a break since my helper has deserted me."

"Mention chocolate chip cookies and my son is a lost cause."

"This guy isn't much different. Where are those cookies?"

"Have a seat on the patio. I'll bring you a plate, if there are any left, and some lemonade."

"You tell Peter if I don't have my share of cookies there will be extra laps at practice."

Rebecca laughed as she went into the house. "I doubt that will make a bit of difference."

"That's what I was afraid of."

In the kitchen Rebecca quickly retrieved two tall glasses from the cabinet and filled them with ice. She noticed her son had taken, by her estimate, at least six cookies and gone off by himself to enjoy them. Peter must be protecting his territory.

After she placed the tray with the cookies and lemonades in the middle of the patio table, she sat across from Gabriel, who rested his head on the bright yellow cushion, his eyes closed, his legs spread as though he was exhausted.

"Tired?" Rebecca took a sip of lemonade.

He pried one eye open and said, "It's hard work trying to maintain an image in front of an impressionable boy. I don't want him to spread the word around town about how inept I am at putting together anything."

"You can always bribe him with your share of chocolate chip cookies."

Gabriel sat up, shaking his head. "Can't do that. I guess I will just have to suffer the slings and arrows of my fellow townspeople."

"Have you had any success in getting Peter to play on the team?"

Gabriel took a bite of cookie, leaving only half of it. "We're gonna practice some later. He's getting a lot better. When he feels comfortable enough, he'll play. I've seen him study the batters. I think he wants to try but is afraid of making a fool of himself."

"Not too different from his coach."

"Hey, I take offense at that remark." He popped the last half of the cookie into his mouth and washed it down with some lemonade. "I'm gonna have to tell Rose she has outdone herself with these cookies."

"She'll love hearing that. Cooking is one of her favorite things. Actually I think that's who I got my love of cooking from. My mother never enjoyed even the simplest task in the kitchen."

"Do you get to cook much?"

"Are you kidding? Granny barely lets me into her private culinary retreat."

"You can always come over to my house and practice. Wouldn't want you to lose your touch."

"And you'd get a home-cooked meal."

"Yep. Can't blame a guy for trying any way he can."

"I might just take you up on that offer."

He leaned forward and snatched another cookie off the plate. "When?"

Suddenly an underlying tension weaved its way into their exchange. "Well." She fumbled in her mind for an answer. "I don't know."

"We could call it a date." He slanted a look at her that melted her insides.

Thankfully she was sitting or she was afraid she

would have collapsed. "A date?" She squeaked the words.

"Yes. You know, where a man and a woman go out together to get to know each other."

"One of those," she murmured. She hadn't had a date in over twelve years. She wasn't sure how one was conducted anymore.

"Of course, I know it's a bit unorthodox to have your date cook dinner, but I'm sure it's done in some circles."

"You don't know?" she asked, purposefully putting a teasing note in her voice. She needed to lighten the mood quickly.

"I haven't dated in fourteen years."

"I haven't in twelve. So we'll be the blind leading the blind."

"Should be an interesting date."

"Okay, for argument's sake, say I accept this date."

"There's no argument here," he said with a grin and a wink.

She threw him a frown to quiet him. "If you'll let me finish. What do you like to eat?"

"Just about anything I don't have to fix."

"So if I prepare liver and onions, you'll be happy and eat every little bite?"

"Just about anything except liver and onions. The onions I don't mind, but the liver I can pass on."

"You know you really aren't helping me. Let me rephrase the question. What is your favorite food?"

He tapped his chin with his forefinger and looked

skyward as though he were in deep thought. "Nothing beats a thick T-bone steak."

"Grilling is the man's job."

"How about I grill the steaks and you fix everything else—whatever you want? Surprise me."

She narrowed her eyes, pretending to consider his proposition carefully. "This might be my time to get back at you for that challenge you won when we went fishing."

His grin widened. "I'm banking on your sweet nature and the fact I'm the town's police chief."

Rebecca couldn't resist the laughter bubbling inside her. Since meeting Gabriel, she had smiled and laughed more than she had in two years. "Okay, I guess you have me over a barrel."

"Now, that's a sight I need to think on."

"What sight, Coach?" Peter pushed open the back door and came outside.

Rebecca started brushing cookie crumbs off her son's chest and face.

"Ah, Mom." Peter tried to step away.

Rebecca grabbed his arm and held him still. "I don't mind you eating the cookies, but I do mind you wearing them."

Peter stood next to her while she finished her task, but his arms and feet didn't stop fidgeting.

"How about me? Do I have any crumbs on my face?"

The teasing tone in Gabriel's voice made her blush. She shot him an exasperated look. "You have a smudge of chocolate right here." She reached out and wiped some from the corner of his mouth with her finger.

Gabriel blinked, surprised by her action. The teasing gleam faded from his gaze to be replaced with astonishment and something else Rebecca didn't want to analyze.

"Coach, ready to go back to work?"

Gabriel shook his head, trying to rid his mind of one recurring thought. Her touch was dynamite. Maybe he should eat another cookie and leave chocolate on his face.

"Coach?" Peter waved his hand in front of Gabriel's face.

Gabriel blinked again. "Oh, sorry. Just thinking. Ready to work?"

"If I'm not mistaken, Granny is expecting you to stay for dinner, unless you would rather eat alone at home," Rebecca said while she gathered up the plate and glasses.

"Nah. If you all insist, I'll stay. It's a dirty job, but someone has to do it."

"The way Josh eats, it certainly is a dirty job." Rebecca headed for the back door.

Gabriel watched her leave, a warmth mellowing him when he thought about their earlier bantering. He hadn't done that in a long time. He had forgotten what it was like to flirt with a beautiful woman and for her to flirt back.

"Hey, Coach, ready?"

"Yes, Peter, I am."

He clasped the boy around his shoulders and

walked with him to where the pieces of doghouse littered the yard. Spending the day with Peter confirmed how much he wished he were a father. He wished he were Peter and Josh's father. That realization snatched his next breath, leaving him struggling for air. He had always been involved in children's lives, but with these two boys he had taken it a step further. Was Rebecca the reason?

"What should we do next, Coach?"

Gabriel focused on what needed to be done. "Let's get all the walls up, then take a look at that roof."

"When we're finished, I want to paint the house."

"What color?" Gabriel cocked his head as though that would help him read the directions better.

"I guess since Peepers is a girl, let's paint it something girly. I can't see pink, though. How about yellow?"

"Sounds good to me." Gabriel held the directions at arm's length then brought them close. He knew they weren't written in a foreign language, but it sure did seem like it when he was trying to figure out what they meant by place knob A into notch D. He wished he had paid more attention in shop.

"You know, Coach, I've been thinking about Miss Bess and the people at the nursing home."

"That's great." Maybe if he held the directions upside down they would make sense.

"I think the team should volunteer once a week to read to the old people there. What do you think?"

"Old people?" Gabriel turned his attention to Peter.

"Yeah, I was thinking we could each adopt a grandmother or grandfather and read to them or play a game with them. I thought I would adopt Miss Bess. She needs me. She reminds me of Granny, and Granny has us. Miss Bess needs us, too."

Gabriel's throat thickened. A month before Peter had been angry at the world. Now he was starting to look at other people's needs and problems and coming up with solutions that made a lot of sense. Gabriel had read somewhere that the more connections a person had, the longer the person would live.

What would happen if suddenly he lost this family? That was a question he never wanted to discover the answer to. He realized he had come to depend on them to feel needed.

Gabriel swallowed several times and said, "Sounds like a doable plan to me."

"Then you don't mind if I say something to David and the others at practice on Monday?"

"Go right ahead. I'll let you organize it, and if you need anyone to help, ask for a volunteer."

"I think David will. I'll call him tonight and ask him if he's interested."

Gabriel wadded the directions into a ball and tossed them toward the trash pile. He could understand his brother-in-law's frustration when he tried to put his niece's dollhouse together last Christmas. Gabriel would never say another word to the man about how hard could it be to put a little old house together. Nope, not a word.

"Tell you what, Peter, let's take a break and practice some ball for a while. When we come back, we'll put our two heads together and come up with a way to finish this doghouse.''

"Are you sure?" Peter scanned the lumber scattered across the yard.

"No, but don't tell anyone I don't have the foggiest idea what I'm doing when it comes to tools. However, I have faith we can manage something. Peepers will need a place to sleep. Rest assured, the Lord will provide a bed—'' he glanced at the walls of the doghouse ''—of sorts.''

"Do you need anything in here?" Rebecca asked Bess as they walked toward the drugstore on Main Street the following Saturday.

"Some hair dye."

"Of course. How long has it been since you dyed your hair?"

"Oh, ages. My dark hair is starting to show."

Rebecca held the door for Bess. "Dark hair? Isn't that what you want?"

Bess headed for the aisle where the dyes were and homed in on the silver. "I refuse to fight Mother Nature. Years ago when I noticed my hair turning gray, I decided to help it along. I dye it every few months to keep the nice silver look, but with everything happening lately I've not kept up."

Rebecca chuckled. The more she was around Bess, the more she liked the way the woman looked at life. She didn't always make sense, but when she did, it was beautiful.

"Ladies, what brings you out on a Saturday afternoon? I saw your car parked out front, Rebecca, and decided to check on my two favorite ladies.''

''Why, Chief Stone, what a nice surprise.'' Bess's eyes twinkled, and her face wrinkled into a bright smile. ''Peepers is enjoying her new house.''

''Then it's still standing?''

''Why wouldn't it be? You made it.''

''Just checking.''

Rebecca rolled her eyes. She had seen what Gabriel and her son had gone through. She wouldn't disillusion Bess on Gabriel's ability at carpentry. But the test would come when the first thunderstorm hit, which shouldn't be too far in the future.

Gabriel followed Bess to the cashier, and Rebecca followed Gabriel. He glanced at her and smiled as though he was giving her a private greeting. Rebecca felt the heat in her cheeks and was glad when Bess said something to distract him.

''We were about to get something to drink at the café. Care to join us, Chief Stone?''

''Only if you call me Gabriel, Bess.''

''I like calling you Chief Stone.''

He nodded. ''Then by all means do.''

They walked the few steps to the diner next door, and Gabriel held the door open while Rebecca and Bess entered. In the middle of the afternoon, the café was deserted except for one customer who was finishing his coffee and a piece of pie.

Bess paused and watched the man slide the last bit of pie into his mouth. ''That's what I want. I love desserts. The more calories and fat there is, the better it is.'' She sat in the nearest chair and waved for the waitress.

''Young lady, I'll have a large piece of pecan pie with vanilla ice cream on top. Now, no skimpy slice for me.'' Bess wagged her finger at the waitress. ''And I'll have some hot tea, too, with a slice of lemon and honey.''

After Rebecca and Gabriel ordered iced tea minus any slices of pie, Bess sighed and placed her purse carefully on the floor next to her chair. Then she took off her white gloves and laid them beside her fork and napkin, one on top of the other. The waitress returned almost immediately with their orders.

''You know, Rebecca, a piece of pie would fill in a few of those curves. I always found curves draw a man's attention.''

Rebecca almost choked on her swallow of tea. The liquid went down the wrong way, and she tried to catch her breath. Gabriel pounded on her back. Her eyes watered as she coughed. Slowly she managed to draw air into her lungs.

He leaned close to Rebecca and whispered, ''So does nearly choking to death.''

Rebecca sent him a *be quiet* look and returned her attention to the older woman across from her. ''Thanks, I'll remember that, Bess.'' She squeaked the words out in a breathy voice.

''Just trying to help. Those boys of yours need a father, especially Peter. Such a fine boy.''

''But they—''

Bess waved her words away. ''Don't tell me they already have one. Rose told me, and he doesn't count. He's never around. Peter told me about his birthday.''

"He did?" Rebecca asked, stunned. Her son wasn't one to open up to just anyone. She knew Peter had visited Bess several times, but she hadn't known they'd become confidants.

"Of course, he did. We talk about everything. Your boys need someone right here in Oakview." Bess cut a large bite of pie, popped it into her mouth and chewed slowly, closing her eyes as though savoring every delicious bit of the dessert. Then she took a sip of tea.

Rebecca heard her stomach rumble. She licked her lips and wished she could enjoy a dessert. But just being in the same room with such a rich pie could add pounds to her body, Rebecca thought with a last wistful look at the near empty plate in front of Bess.

Bess pointed her fork at Gabriel. "And, Chief Stone, you've been alone long enough. You're too good a man to waste. Get back into the thick of things.''

"Bess, I am—"

"No, you aren't. You still wear your wedding ring. That screams 'Do not approach, taken,' to any woman interested." Bess ate another bite of her dessert, smacking her lips. "This will certainly go right to my hips, but then at my age I don't have to worry. By the time the fat could kill me, I'll be dead anyway. One of the advantages to being old."

Rebecca felt Gabriel's astonished gaze on her. She was afraid to look at the man. She was sure her face was beet red. Bess had forgotten what the word tact meant.

"So when are you two going out on a date?"

Gabriel nearly spewed his tea all over the table. He managed to recover quicker than Rebecca did, but his eyes were wide and his mouth hung open slightly.

"Chief?" Bess quirked a brow at him. "I never took you to be a foolish man."

Rebecca glanced at her watch. "Oh, look at the time, Bess. I have to get you back to Shady Oaks."

"I'm not leaving until I finish this last bite and get an answer to my question." Bess stared hard at Gabriel.

"Bess, Rebecca and I already have a date."

"We do?" Rebecca said before she realized Bess would pounce on that comment.

"Remember last weekend when I was building the doghouse and we talked on the patio?"

"When are you going out?"

"Tomorrow night," Gabriel said.

At the same time Rebecca answered, "Sometime soon."

Bess arched a brow. "Which is it?"

Rebecca peered at Gabriel and let him get them out of this mess. "Rebecca, will you go out with me tomorrow night?"

"But I haven't shopped for any of the food I'll need."

"Ah, are you going to cook him something to eat? My mother always said the way to a man's heart was through his stomach, and my Ralph certainly proved her right.''

''I'll meet you at the grocery store after you take Bess home.''

''Well, in that case, Rebecca, let's shake a leg. You've got plans to make.''

''We don't have to go out,'' Rebecca said as she walked next to the shopping cart Gabriel pushed down the meat aisle. ''We probably need to put our foot down or Bess will think she can manipulate us into doing anything she wants.''

''I'm not arguing with this plan.'' He grinned. ''I get a home-cooked meal out of it. Why should I disagree.''

''I know I should take offense, but I get to cook a meal—finally.''

''So we both get what we want.''

''Just two happy campers.''

''Right.'' Gabriel stopped at the case that held the steaks and carefully inspected each package before placing one in the cart. ''I have my part. Where do you want to go?''

''The produce section first.''

As Rebecca strolled next to Gabriel, she couldn't shake the feeling that their relationship was shifting, whether it was Bess's doing or not. Yes, friends cooked for each other, but this felt as if they were more than friends. She should put a stop to this date before things got out of hand, before Bess did something else to throw them together. But she wanted to cook for Gabriel. She loved to cook, and Craig never had appreciated her efforts. For some reason she felt Gabriel would be different, and she needed that.

"Well, isn't this a surprise?" Alicia nearly locked carts with Gabriel when they rounded a corner simultaneously from opposite directions. "Shopping together? Anything I should know about?"

"Not if we don't want the whole town to know before the sun goes down," Gabriel replied, stepping to maneuver around Alicia.

"Gabriel Stone, I do not gossip."

Both Gabriel's eyebrows shot up. "That's news to me."

"Okay, so I like to talk a little. But no one will hear about this from me." Alicia started down the aisle.

Gabriel watched Alicia disappear. "Don't count on that, Rebecca. Tomorrow in church, I'm afraid, you'll be inundated with questions about us."

"Just me?" She ignored the words *about us*. It made them sound like a couple.

"No, I'm afraid I will, too." Gabriel headed for the checkout.

"I keep forgetting how small towns are. Will the gossip bother you?" She wasn't sure how she felt about being linked with Gabriel romantically. No, that wasn't quite the truth. She was terrified because she was starting to care a great deal about the man, and she didn't think he was ready for another commitment. She wasn't sure she could handle another commitment emotionally after Craig had hurt her so badly. And she was positive she didn't want her children to suffer anymore.

"I'm a man in the public eye. Gossip follows me."

"It does? I haven't heard a word of it."

"You mean you haven't heard about Calvin and me? Or Annie and me?"

Rebecca put their items on the checkout counter. "No, what about them?"

"Oh, nothing." Gabriel took out his wallet to pay the cashier.

Rebecca was aware of the young woman behind the counter listening intently to their conversation. Rebecca refrained from saying another word until they were outside. She followed Gabriel to his Jeep, handing him bags to place inside. He closed the back door, then went to the driver's side.

Rebecca stopped him with a hand on his arm. "Oh, no, you don't. You can't casually mention some little tidbit then not say another word. I'm human and I want to know about Calvin and Annie."

"It isn't about Calvin and Annie. It's about Calvin and me and Annie and me. Two separate stories." He grinned and slid behind the steering wheel. "Two stories I'll save until we have dinner tomorrow night." He started the engine and backed out of the parking space, leaving her standing in front of the grocery store.

Who was Annie? It was all Rebecca could think about as she drove home. When she pulled into her driveway, she was determined to have the answers before tomorrow night. No one knew the townspeople better than her grandmother.

* * *

Well, Granny had been able to tell her who Calvin was, but Annie was still a mystery. Rebecca approached Gabriel's front door. The warm evening air with a hint of mowed grass permeating the light breeze reminded her that summer wasn't far away. She pushed the bell and listened to it chime, tapping her foot on the wooden porch. Calvin had turned out to be a farmer outside town who had a habit of shooting at anyone who came onto his property—until Gabriel cured him.

But who was Annie?

The door swung open, and Gabriel filled the entryway. "Right on time." He looked around her. "Did you walk?"

She nodded. "It's hard to pass up a day like today. Summer will be here all too fast, and with it the heat. I like to take advantage of the nice weather when I can." She stepped inside his house. "Okay, I'm here. Who is Annie?"

He laughed. "You know about Calvin and me?"

"He could have hurt you."

"I knew he wouldn't."

"How?"

Gabriel shrugged. "Just did."

"But to keep walking toward him as he shot at you? I'm sure that isn't in the police chief manual."

"I wasn't the police chief at the time, but I think the good people of Oakview felt they had to give me the job after that incident."

"Yeah, anyone crazy enough to let someone shoot at them must be crazy enough to be a police chief."

"Right. Someone had to call the old man's bluff. Besides, he was shooting at the dirt around me."

Rebecca walked toward the kitchen. "Okay, now that we know about Calvin, what about Annie? Did this involve a gun, too?"

"Oh, no. Annie couldn't have held a gun if she had wanted to—which I doubt she would have, since she was a cow."

"A cow!" That certainly wasn't the picture she had conjured up on the walk to his house. Rebecca pivoted toward Gabriel and saw the amusement deep in his eyes.

"Of course, at the time I knew her she was a calf, and I was her rescuer." He swept his arm wide. "My kitchen is your kitchen." He started for the back door.

"Hold it! How did you rescue her?"

Gabriel came to a stop and turned slowly toward Rebecca. "The story would be better on a full stomach."

She fisted her hands on her hips. "There will be no full stomach if there's no story."

"Blackmailing me? The town's police chief?"

"You bet."

He lounged against the counter. "There really isn't much to tell. Annie got stuck in a bog, and I had to get her out. Of course, after she got out, I ended up stuck in the bog up to my thighs and had to wait for help to arrive—three hours later. Not one of my finer moments, if you ask me. I think I was the punch line for a few jokes after that."

Rebecca pressed her lips together, but the corners

of her mouth twitched. Finally she couldn't contain her laughter any longer. "You mean Annie didn't go for help?" she asked, wiping the tears from her eyes.

"Actually she did wander back to her owner, but sadly she couldn't say where she had been."

Her laughter settled into a huge smile. "Life in a small town is certainly different from a big city. I can't say I ever heard of that happening to the police chief of Dallas. But then I doubt he got out much."

"I'm a hands-on type of guy. I wouldn't want to be stuck behind a desk."

"As opposed to being stuck in a bog?" The laughter bubbled up again, and she found herself unable to stop. She collapsed into a chair at the table, picturing him with mud up to his thighs, trying to take a step forward and unable to.

He waited until she ceased and said, "I'm glad you find the situation amusing."

"You don't?"

A smile cracked the stern expression on his face. "Now I do. Not at the time. All I wanted to do was slink home and not come out for days."

"Were you able to?"

"No. I had a steady parade of people pay me visits that evening on one pretext after another. The only things they really wanted to know, however, were the gory details."

"Which you supplied?"

"Yes. It was either me or the person who found me, and I didn't want her to."

"Who?"

"Mabel."

"You're kidding? That's rich. She pulled you out?"

"You have to remember she was in the Navy once, and she's quite strong for a small woman."

Rebecca held up her hand. "Okay. Okay. I don't think I want any more details. I'll just let my imagination work overtime."

"That's what I'm afraid you'll do." He pushed away from the counter. "Have fun with it. I'm starting the fire."

When the door closed behind Gabriel, she moved toward the refrigerator to get the ingredients for twice-baked potatoes and broccoli-cheese casserole. While she washed the potatoes, she spied Gabriel on the patio, cleaning the barbecue.

Since she had met him, she had laughed more than in the past few years. He enjoyed life and lived it to the fullest. His faith had sustained him through difficult times and made him a stronger man. As she observed him fill the pit with fresh charcoal, she couldn't deny her feelings any longer. She was falling in love with Gabriel Stone.

Chapter Ten

"**Y**ou may cook for me anytime. You have a gift." Gabriel wiped his mouth with his napkin and folded it next to his plate.

Rebecca's hand shook as she picked up her glass and drank cool water. All she had been able to think about during dinner was that she had fallen in love with Gabriel. And she knew neither of them was ready for another commitment. She wanted a total commitment from a man. He had to love her for herself, not the ready-made family she would give him. If Gabriel could commit, would it be for the right reasons?

"I'm glad you liked my food," she finally murmured after putting the glass on the patio table.

"Especially your dessert. Your chocolate eclairs were wonderful, mouthwatering, rich—"

She chuckled. "I get the picture. You can have the last one."

He pounced on it, taking his time devouring it, a

huge grin on his face. He licked every morsel of chocolate off his fingertips. Transfixed, Rebecca watched. How was she going to protect her heart? She knew it was too late. Gabriel wouldn't mean to hurt her, but make no mistake, she would be hurt. He was an honorable person who would realize a commitment had to be based on love between the man and woman, not on the fact he wanted a family.

Gabriel stretched his long legs in front of him and relaxed in his chair. "I don't think I'm gonna be able to move for a while."

Rebecca looked up and noticed some clouds racing across the moon. She took a deep breath and smelled rain in the air. "I think a storm's building."

He rested his head on the cushion and stared at the darkening sky. "That might not be good news for Peepers. Thank goodness she'll be inside with Bess tonight if it does storm."

"It's bound to happen during the daytime. Then what?"

"Pray, and if that doesn't work, buy a doghouse ready made, which is what I should have done in the first place."

"But you wanted to spend some time with Peter."

He raised his head and fixed his gaze on her. "Was I that obvious?"

"No, I don't think Peter suspected a thing. Even if he did, he loved every minute of you two building that—doghouse."

"You're too kind. I'm not sure that's what I'd call the thing we built."

"Mothers look at their children's creations with rose-colored glasses."

Gabriel laughed. "At least I got some good news out of him while we worked. He told me he wants to join the team as a player and participate in our next game. He wants to start working out with the others at practice. Actually he already has, to some extent."

"Now I'm really gonna be nervous when I watch the games. It's so much easier when your child is the manager. No pressure."

"But it's so much more exciting when he hits the ball and gets a run."

"Do you think he has a chance?"

"Yes. I'm his coach. He's more than ready. He was from the beginning, but Peter feels he must be perfect in order to be valuable to the team."

"It's because of his dad. Craig always pushed Peter to do everything perfectly. If he didn't, Craig wouldn't say anything to encourage him, or he would make sure Peter knew everything he had done wrong."

Gabriel straightened, all casualness gone from his expression. He clenched his jaw, and his hands curled tightly around the arms of the wrought iron chair. "Is that why Peter's afraid to try anything new?"

Rebecca nodded, afraid to speak for fear her voice would crack.

"I've been trying to get him to join the children's choir. He keeps telling me he doesn't sing very well, but I've heard him. He has a beautiful voice."

"You've gotten him to do more than I thought you would be able to. Give him time. He'll come around."

"He has all the time in the world with me. I'm not going anywhere. Some day he'll realize that."

But I might have to go somewhere else, especially when it becomes too painful to be around you and not be fully a part of your life. She immediately pushed the thought of moving into the background, not wanting to put a damper on the evening. "I'm glad you care for my son."

"I care for both your sons, Rebecca. They're important to me."

"The family you never had," she said before she realized the meaning of what she was saying.

Gabriel flinched as though struck.

"I realize you always wanted a large family. With your wife's death that was taken away from you." She sat forward, deciding to broach the subject that had been bothering her since she realized her feelings for Gabriel were deepening. "Are you using my sons as a substitute for the family you lost?"

"You don't pull any punches, do you?"

Rebecca rose, restless. "I try not to anymore. I did once. I'm beginning to care for you as more than a friend." She pivoted toward him. "I don't want to be hurt again. I won't be the only one to suffer. My boys will, too."

Gabriel surged to his feet and covered the distance between them but kept his arms at his sides. "I would never hurt you or the boys. Never."

"Not intentionally. But—" Rebecca reached out

and clasped his left hand "—things turn out in ways we never intended."

"I'm not going to kid you, Rebecca. Yes, I wanted a family with lots of children with Judy. And I still want that family. I have never tried to hide that fact from anyone who knows me."

"But can you love the woman who will ultimately bear your children as she needs to be loved?" Rebecca ran her finger over his wedding ring. "Can you move on?"

He looked at their hands. "I don't know." He brought his troubled gaze to hers. "That's the best answer I can give you right now."

"Then that's the only one I want. I want no lies between us. I've had that. Never again."

"Give me time." He lifted his hand and stroked his thumb across her lips.

The first drop of rain splattered Rebecca's head. She glanced up, and another splashed her forehead. "We'd better get these dishes inside before it really starts to pour."

Gabriel cupped her face and peered into her eyes. "You're special, Rebecca Michaels." Combing his fingers through her hair, he lowered his mouth toward hers.

The sky opened, releasing a deluge of water and forcing them apart. Rebecca hurried toward the table to grab as many dishes as she could. Gabriel stopped her and pulled her toward the house.

"I'll get them when it stops."

"Are you sure?" she asked as the back door

slammed. She turned to look out and could hardly see the table.

"Very," Gabriel said close to her ear.

The tickle of his breath caused goose bumps to rise on her skin. She stepped away. "It looks like it'll rain for a while. I think I need to bum a ride home."

"It's early."

"But tomorrow's a workday, and I need to make sure Peter has his homework done."

"I think you planned this to get out of doing the dishes."

"Clever, wasn't I? But then all you have to do is let the rain do your job for you."

He glanced out the window. "If they aren't washed away." He grasped her hand. "Come on. Let's dig up an umbrella and get you home."

Several days later Rebecca eased the door to the police station open and peeked in to see if Mabel was at her desk. Sighing heavily, she quietly shut the door and knelt by Josh, who was in his stroller.

She ran her fingers through his baby-fine hair. "I know Gabriel said to come on and bring you in today, but—" Drawing in a deep, fortifying breath, she stood. "I have to get my courage up. I was hoping to get here early enough to sneak you past Mabel. No such luck. I think the woman sleeps at the station."

"No, but she sure beats me most mornings."

Rebecca gasped and whirled to find Gabriel lounging against the door with his arms crossed and a smile on his face. His eyes made a leisurely trek up her body. "Good morning, you two."

"Are you sure this will be okay? I know Mabel took good care of Josh at the church nursery, but you know how she feels about the workplace."

"If you hadn't been able to bring Josh with you to work, would you have stayed home?"

"Yes."

"Then that's the tactic we take with her. Your grandmother isn't feeling well, and your neighbor, Ann, is in Tulsa for the week. You don't have anyone to take care of Josh."

"Maybe Alicia—"

"Stop. This will work out. I promise. And I never renege on a promise."

She offered him a tentative smile. "That's one of the things I like about you. Lead the way."

Gabriel opened the door for Rebecca. Mabel glanced up from the keyboard and frowned. Then Josh cooed, and her frown dissolved into a smile. She rose, crossed the room and scooped Josh into her arms.

"Is your grandmother sick?" Mabel asked, blowing softly on Josh to get him to laugh.

"Her sinuses are really bothering her, and she has a bad headache."

"Well, I see we won't get much work done today," Mabel murmured to Josh and carried him to her desk. She sat with him in her lap.

"I think someone kidnapped Mabel Preston," Rebecca whispered to Gabriel.

"I knew she liked children, but if this doesn't beat all."

Rebecca wasn't sure what to do. She stared at Mabel while the woman explained to Josh the inner workings of the computer.

Mabel looked up. "At least one of us should get busy."

And in Rebecca's mind she knew exactly to whom Mabel was referring. Rebecca pushed the stroller to her desk and parked it next to her chair. She hurriedly began logging in the incident reports from the evening before. Thankfully there weren't many.

When she was through, she peered at Mabel. The woman and her baby were gone. Rebecca leaped to her feet and searched the large room. Then she noticed the door to the courthouse was ajar. She went in pursuit of them and found Mabel showing off Josh to several of the secretaries in the building.

"You need to let others enjoy your son as much as you do." Gabriel came up behind her.

"But he's..."

"Disabled?"

She nodded.

"Is that any reason someone couldn't love him? When I look at Josh, I see a child with the sweetest face and the biggest brown eyes. He's so trusting and innocent. As an officer of the law I forget sometimes what that means, and he always reminds me."

Rebecca went into the police station. She felt adrift, even though she had work to do.

"I'm going to see Ben at his store. It seems someone is shoplifting again."

"At least Bess is in the clear."

"Thank goodness. He thinks it's some teenage girls who were in the store last night. He feels they're putting pressure on each other to shoplift."

"I hope I won't have to deal with that. I know how difficult peer pressure can be. Thanks to you, Peter's getting to know some good kids. David was over at the house yesterday after school. They did their homework together, then practiced some baseball."

"The kids your child hangs with are important. I'm glad I could help." Gabriel paused at the door. "When I get back, I want to take you and Josh on a picnic at lunchtime. The day's too beautiful to eat inside."

Before Rebecca realized it, it was almost one. Josh was stirring from his nap in his stroller, where she'd placed him while Mabel went to lunch. Through the doorway, Rebecca saw Gabriel hang up the phone and rise from his desk. Mabel was back. Excitement tingled through her.

He came out of his office. "Ready to go?"

She nodded and finished what she was entering on the computer. "Are we walking?"

"Yep. The park is down the block. On the way I want to stop at the diner and pick up the food I ordered."

"So the diner does picnic lunches," Mabel said, bending over the stroller to smile at Josh and touch his cheek.

"Nope, not usually. They're doing me a favor."

"Oh, boss, I don't know if that's a good idea."

Mabel straightened, winked at Rebecca, then turned to Gabriel, presenting a stern facade. "What will the townspeople think of you, currying favors like that?"

"I insisted on paying extra for the picnic lunch."

Mabel punched Gabriel in the shoulder playfully. "I'll tell you what they'll think. That it's about time you came to your senses and started dating again."

"But—" Gabriel cleared his throat.

Rebecca's cheeks reddened. "This isn't—"

"Are you two pretending you aren't dating? If so, it isn't working. I've heard through the grapevine that you've already been on your first official date last Sunday night."

Gabriel and Rebecca looked at each other. "Bess!"

"Did you really think you'd keep it a secret in a town like Oakview?" Mabel shook her head, tsking. "Boss, you should know better than that. If you want, I can keep Josh while you two go eat lunch."

"That's okay. I'm sure you have a lot of work to do," Rebecca said, gripping the handle of the stroller as though Mabel would rip it out of her hands.

"If I don't get through, I'll stay this evening until I finish."

"I can't let you do that." Rebecca glanced at Gabriel for some help. He shrugged.

"What do I have to do at home? I live by myself with no obligations."

The loneliness Rebecca heard in Mabel's voice stirred her compassion. Until that moment Rebecca hadn't thought of Mabel as being lonely. "If you're sure—"

"Go. Enjoy your lunch. Josh and I have some serious talking to do." Mabel took the stroller and headed for her desk before Rebecca changed her mind.

Outside the police station, Rebecca paused and looked in through the picture window at Mabel taking Josh out of the stroller and holding him close to her. The whole time the woman was talking to Josh as if he understood every word she was saying. Rebecca's heart expanded, and she fought the emotions threatening her composure.

"I was so wrong about Mabel. Did you hear her teasing you in there?" Rebecca asked.

Gabriel placed his hand at the small of her back. "Mabel never married, but she has lots of nieces and nephews. Most of them live in other parts of Oklahoma and Texas, but the ones who live here she dotes on. I think she's just adopted your son as another of her charges."

"Speaking of adopting, I suppose you're aware of Peter adopting Bess as his grandmother. Did you come up with that idea for the Cougars?"

"Peter didn't tell you?"

"No, what?"

"That adoption scheme was all his idea. He organized the Cougars with David's help. You have quite a son there. Actually you have quite a family." Gabriel stopped outside the diner. "You wait here. I'll get our food."

While he was gone, Rebecca scanned Main Street and noticed a few of the people on the sidewalk staring at her. She waved to them, and they waved back.

One young mother from church paused when she passed Rebecca and told her about a meeting of the young mom's group on Saturday. Clara encouraged Rebecca to join them. As Clara strolled away, Rebecca drew in a deep breath of spring air and thought about how content she felt. In a short time she had become a part of this town, even a part of the church. She had never experienced this feeling of belonging when she lived in Dallas even though she'd lived there over seven years.

"Let's go," Gabriel said, grasping her hand and walking toward the park a block away.

"A basket and everything."

"I told them I wanted only the best."

At the park, Gabriel chose a picnic table under a big oak tree. He opened the basket, and spread a cloth over the stone table. Container after container came out of the basket, and Rebecca's mouth fell open.

"You must have been hungry."

Gabriel glanced at all the food, and a sheepish look entered his eyes. "I guess I went overboard. We can take the leftovers to the station. They won't last long if I put them out for everyone to take some."

"Yes, I noticed the policemen who work for you have hearty appetites. Those cookies Rose baked for them the other day didn't last an hour." Rebecca tilted her head. "Come to think of it, most of them were gone after you were alone with the plate."

Gabriel grinned. "Okay. I confess I probably took more than my share. In my defense, I can only say chocolate does crazy things to me."

"To be fair to the others, I need to tell Granny to bake oatmeal or sugar cookies next time."

Gabriel produced two large slices of the diner's famous French silk pie. "Well, in that case I ought to eat both of these."

Rebecca snatched a plate from his hand. "I don't think so." She put it out of his reach on the bench next to her.

She filled a plastic plate with fried chicken, potato salad, coleslaw and a roll with butter dripping off it. Gabriel sat across from her and piled his plate even higher.

After a bite of chicken, he said, "Next to home cooking—" his gaze caught hers "—yours in particular, this is the best food around these parts."

She laughed. "Okay. You must want something. You're buttering me up more than these rolls are. Spit it out, Stone."

"Another home-cooked meal would be greatly appreciated. And—" he picked up a paper cup of iced tea "—I would love to have you sing the solo at next week's service."

Rebecca dropped her plastic fork. "Sing in front of the whole church by myself?"

"That's what solo means." He leaned over, his expression intense, and seized the hand that had been holding the fork. "You've got a beautiful voice. I want everyone to hear how beautiful it is."

"But I can't—"

Gabriel held up his free hand. "Hold it. Don't say no yet. Think about it. What better way to celebrate what God has given you than by celebrating Him with a song?''

There was a part of her that wanted to accept the invitation, but there was a part that was afraid, that still wasn't sure where she stood with her faith. How could she celebrate God when she had doubts? ''I'll think about it, Gabriel. Please give me more time.''

His grasp on her hand tightened for a moment before he released his hold. ''Rebecca, you have all the time in the world. I'll never force you to do anything you don't want to. You just say the word, and I'll give you the floor.'' He took a bite of his roll and chewed slowly, his regard fixed upon her face.

She dropped her gaze to her plate, feeling his probing look, and searched for a safe topic of conversation. ''I'm picking Bess up this evening and bringing her to Peter's first game as a player. She's quite excited about seeing him play.''

''And Peter's quite excited about playing. He tries not to act like it means anything, but the last two practices he has asked me to stay and pitch to him afterward.''

''I wondered why he was late, but he wouldn't say anything. What if Peter doesn't do well?''

''He'll do fine, Rebecca. I promise.''

''I know you pride yourself on always keeping your word. But Gabriel, you don't have control over this. Peter's the only one.''

''I know your son's abilities. He can do it.''

''But I don't know if he realizes that. I watched my son over the years slowly shut down because Craig demanded perfection.''

"No one is perfect, especially ten-year-old boys."
Again Gabriel's gaze captured hers. "Rebecca,
you're just gonna have to believe in Peter and me.
If he fails, I'll help him through it."

"That's my job," she immediately said.

His look sharpened. "There you go again, not
wanting to share. You're not alone, Rebecca, and the
sooner you realize it the easier things will be for
you." Gabriel spread his arms wide. "You have a
whole town that cares about you."

What about you? Rebecca wanted to ask, but
didn't. She didn't know if she could handle his answer. "I realize I'm not alone."

He lifted a brow. "Do you?"

She straightened on the stone bench. "But I am
Peter's parent."

"And I'm not?"

"You're Peter's coach. Of course, his playing is
your concern, but—" Her words dried up.

"But that will be all I ever am?"

She swallowed around the constriction in her
throat. "I don't want to get into this, Gabriel. We
need to get back. I still have physical therapy exercises to do with Josh." She reached for her pie. Rebecca focused on it rather than the intent look on
Gabriel's face, which incorporated anger as well as
sadness.

Rebecca shifted between Alicia and Bess. Peter
walked to home plate and took a few practice swings.
Rebecca's heartbeat accelerated. Biting her nails
when she was nervous was a habit she had worked

hard to break several years before. When she found herself starting to resort to the old habit, she quickly sat on her hands.

"Oh, isn't this exciting," Bess said in Rebecca's right ear.

Alicia said in her left one, "He's gonna do fine. Don't you worry."

But worry nibbled at Rebecca's composure. She caught her breath as Peter took his first swing and missed. She cringed when the ump shouted, "Strike one." When the ump announced the second strike, she chewed on her lower lip and closed her eyes. She didn't want to see the next pitch. She pried one eye open and saw her son swing at a ball that was outside and too low. The sound of it hitting the catcher's glove reverberated through her mind as the ump's words did. "Strike three. You're out."

She started to rise, to go to her son. Both Alicia and Bess placed a hand on her arms and held her down.

"You don't want to do that, my child," Bess said, pointing to Peter stalking to the dugout with a frown carved deep into his boyish features. "Let the coach handle it."

"But he's hurting."

"It won't be the last time. Gabriel will help him shake it off." Alicia patted Rebecca's arm and released her hold. "I sometimes think this game is harder on the parents than the children playing."

Rebecca watched her son plop down on the bench and hang his head, tuning out everything the other boys said to him. She knew he was drawing in on himself, berating himself for failing. She was afraid he wouldn't try to bat when his next turn came. She wanted to go to him so badly and put her arms around him, hugging him to her and telling him that it would be all right.

When Gabriel knelt in front of Peter and spoke to him, her son looked at his coach, shook his head and straightened on the bench. Peter watched the rest of the batters as they played, then, when the teams changed places, he snatched up his glove and headed for the outfield.

"See? I told you Gabriel knew just what to say to him. He'll be all right."

Rebecca was beginning to believe Alicia might be right about her son. She settled in for a long evening.

"Is this Josh?" Clara asked.

Nodding, Rebecca prepared herself for the questions that usually followed.

"He's adorable. As I told you earlier, you should join us for the young mom's group on Saturday and bring him to play with the others. We don't leave our children at home. They're a part of the group, too."

Rebecca started to say no, but the word wouldn't come out.

"That would be perfect, Rebecca."

Rebecca shot Bess a bewildered look. Perfect? "Josh doesn't play much," she finally said to the woman in front of her.

"We have all ages ranging from a few months to four-and five-year-olds. Alicia can tell you all about it." The woman patted Josh's cap-covered head, then made her way to her husband who was sitting a few rows back and to the left.

"You know, I think she's right. The young mom's group would be great for you. It would give you a chance to get involved with the church. They do all kinds of projects, from sponsoring a huge garage sale every spring to a carnival in the fall to raise money for the Sunday school."

"I'll have to think about it. I need to start Josh in some more therapy in Tulsa, and Saturday may be my only day to do it."

As the game progressed, Rebecca reflected on her changing role as a working mother. She would like to join the group, but she didn't know if she had the time to do that, take care of Josh's therapy, be a mother to Peter and hold down a full-time job. She was finding there was only so much time in a day.

When Peter stepped up to bat two innings later, Rebecca felt the tension in her neck. She'd seen Gabriel whisper something to her eldest, pat him on the back and send him out. Again Peter swung at the first pitch and missed. He looked at Gabriel, who gave him a thumbs-up sign.

A light, cool breeze ruffled her hair. Sweat was rolling down her face, stinging her eyes and leaving salty tracks. Rebecca breathed deeply to ease the pounding of her heart and watched as Peter tapped his bat against home plate then positioned himself.

Peter hit the ball, and it went sailing into the outfield. He ran toward first. Pumping his legs as hard as he could, he rounded first and headed for second, then on to third, sliding into the base as the ball was caught by the third baseman.

"Safe," the ump called, and Rebecca jumped to her feet, screaming and clapping.

When she sat again, she noticed all the spectators' eyes were on her and she flushed, then shrugged and said, "That's my son."

Everyone applauded her and smiled.

She was tempted to bow but didn't. She sat, feeling the heat on her cheeks. She caught Gabriel staring at her, and her blush deepened. His grin widened and he winked, giving her a thumbs-up.

"Okay, restraint isn't one of my virtues."

"I like it," Alicia said. "I personally like an excuse to act like a maniac every once in a while. Very therapeutic, if you ask me. Just wait until David comes to bat."

When the game was over, Rebecca asked Bess to watch Josh for a moment while she headed for the group of boys. She wanted to comfort Peter. The Cougars had lost, and she was worried he would blame himself. She paused a few feet away and listened as Gabriel congratulated the team on playing a good game. Then he had them bow their heads while he said a prayer of thanks to God.

"Practice next Monday after school. See you all at Pizza To Go in a few minutes," Gabriel announced to the team, then clasped Peter by the shoulder while the rest of the boys filed away. "I'm pleased by your first performance. Four times at bat. One triple and another single."

"But I struck out twice."

"Remember, focus on the positive. No one—professional ball players included—has a hit every time at bat. You're an asset to the team, Peter. No doubt about it."

Rebecca listened to Gabriel target what Peter had done that was right, not wrong. Peter beamed under Gabriel's attention and words. His small chest puffed out, and he walked with his head held high toward her when Gabriel was through. If Rebecca hadn't seen the game, she would have thought the Cougars had won. No berating and yelling about the mistakes made.

"Did you see my triple, Mom?"

"Yes, I did. Quite a play."

Peter looked around Rebecca toward Bess. "I'll be back in a minute." He raced to the older lady and sat next to her.

Rebecca watched her eldest for a few seconds, then faced Gabriel. "Between Granny and Bess, that guy has all his bases covered as far as grandparents go."

"Speaking of Rose, how is she?"

"Better. She wanted to come tonight, but I'm making her stay home and rest."

"I didn't think anyone could make Rose do anything she didn't want to."

"I promised her I would come by and get her for the pizza. She agreed to the compromise, which tells you she wasn't feeling well at all today. Even Josh is a little fussier these past few days. I hope his ear infection isn't returning. I'm so glad tomorrow is Saturday, and I don't have to work."

"I think I should be upset. After all, I am your boss." Gabriel walked toward home plate to retrieve a bat left by the last player.

Rebecca followed. "Who has work to do when he's at the station. You shouldn't have to spend your day giving Josh physical therapy."

"But I wanted to. There was no emergency I had to go to. Besides, it was only thirty minutes."

"But it's not part of your job description."

"Coming to townspeople's rescue is part of my job."

"I didn't need rescuing."

Gabriel stopped in the middle of the baseball diamond. "Are you so sure about that?"

Rebecca put her hands on her hips. "Gabriel Stone, I am not a fragile woman who needs a man to rescue her."

He laid his hand on her arm. "From where I stand you've lost your way and you're trying to find the path back to God. Am I wrong?"

A tightness in her throat burned and made it difficult to answer him. Finally she said, "Is that the way you see our relationship?" Suddenly she didn't want to hear his response. She pivoted and strode toward her family. She needed to get away before she broke down in front of everyone.

Gabriel grasped her and spun her toward him. "I want to help you not only find God again but find what you want in your life. Until you do, how can there be anything lasting between us? I want to be your friend and—" he sucked in a deep breath "—and more, but your life, and I'm finding my life, aren't settled. We both have issues that make it difficult for us to commit to another.''

She shook his hand off her arm and continued toward her family, desperately wanting to deny his words but knowing he spoke the truth, as usual. Until they got their own separate houses in order, they couldn't become one family.

Chapter Eleven

"Child, what do you think about us working on a quilt for the carnival in the fall?" Granny stopped in front of Rebecca, leaning on her cane.

Rebecca inspected her grandmother's features, glad to see some color in her cheeks after the week she'd spent fighting off her allergies. "You and Bess?" she asked, turning to the older woman.

"And you," Bess added. "I think a quilt with different scenes from the Bible would be perfect for the auction. We could start with Adam and Eve and tell the story of the Old Testament."

"I like that."

"If we start now, we should be through in six months." Granny looked around for a chair, found one and eased into it. "I do declare these old bones creak at times."

Bess took the chair next to Rose. "At least you have a sharp mind. I keep forgetting things I know I shouldn't."

Rebecca left the two ladies talking and went in search of Gabriel, who had taken off with Josh the second she had arrived at the church social. In less than two minutes she found him in the midst of the children on the playground. The stroller was in a corner by the church building. He held Josh in the crook of his arm so her son could see everything that was going on. Gabriel pointed to a group of children playing on the jungle gym, one little boy hanging upside down.

When she walked up to Gabriel, he smiled and said, "We should plan Josh's birthday. Rose told me it was coming up soon."

We? That pronoun more than anything made her heart lurch and her hope soar. She liked the sound of it on his lips, but she had to remind herself not to get too excited. He still wore his wedding ring, which in her mind represented a high wall around his heart and indicated he was not ready to commit to anyone.

"I just thought we would have a quiet family get-together."

"Nonsense. I think we should invite the kids from the church nursery and have a gala event. It's not every day a child has his second birthday."

"Well—"

"Let me plan everything. I thought I did a pretty good job with Peter's."

"Yes, but—" Again her words lodged in her throat.

"Okay?"

"Yes," she finally said, taking her son into her arms and hugging him close. "It's time for his afternoon nap. He's been sleeping more than usual lately. I think he might be trying to catch something. Did you say Mabel was going to be in the nursery?''

"Yep.''

"It's probably better if Josh lies down rather than catnapping in his stroller. I'll be right back.''

Gabriel watched Rebecca enter the church building, a feeling of emptiness engulfing him as she moved away. When she disappeared from sight, he stared at his left hand and the wedding ring he still wore. What was holding him back from removing it? He cared a great deal for Rebecca and her family. He touched his wedding ring and slid it almost all the way off his finger.

A child's laughter penetrated his thoughts, and he slid the ring back on. What if she was right about him only wanting a family? What if his feelings for her weren't the real thing but just a knee-jerk reaction to not having what he wanted most with Judy? He had to be one hundred percent sure before he made any commitment to her. He would not be responsible for hurting her. Rebecca deserved the very best. He wasn't sure he was able to give his best.

Gabriel strode toward the barbecues that were lined up ready to cook hamburgers and hot dogs. Dashing by, Peter waved hello and continued after David and another boy on the Cougar team. Gabriel realized he did love Rebecca's two sons and would hate not being a part of their lives. How did he separate his feelings for her two sons from the feelings he had for their mother? They were a package deal.

"Hey, Gabriel, come settle a little disagreement

for us. We need to know how you arrange your charcoal to get the best fire going,'' the reverend called, gesturing him to a group of men in front of one barbecue.

Gabriel started for them, but a motion out of the corner of his eye caught his attention. He turned toward the movement and froze. George McCall shut his car door, then walked toward the table where the food was set out. He carried a plastic bowl. Gabriel fisted his hands at his sides.

After George placed his bowl of food on the table, he scanned the crowd, avoiding eye contact. Hesitantly George approached two people not far from the table and started talking to them.

Gabriel opened and closed his hands, trying to control his emotions. But he couldn't. Everything faded but George, alive and well, calmly carrying on a conversation as though nothing had happened three years before to destroy Gabriel's life.

He took a step toward George.

Reverend Carson blocked his path. ''Think before you do anything you'll regret.''

''Did you know he was going to be here today?'' Gabriel heard the seething tone of his voice and didn't care. Anger consumed him, with a touch of guilt thrown in.

''Yes, Gabriel, I did. He's a member of this church, too.''

''Why didn't you tell me?''

''Because you wouldn't have come to the social.''

''You're right about that.''

''George intends to be an active member of our

church again. He needs us. He's changed, Gabriel. He hasn't had a drink since the day of the accident.''

Gabriel flexed his hands. His emotions boiled beneath the surface, ready to erupt. "I don't know if I can attend the same church as that man.''

"Forgiveness is important in God's scheme of things. I can't choose between two parishioners. Don't ask me to.''

Gabriel looked at George. The man glanced at him, a cautious expression on his face. "You should have told me he was going to be here, Samuel. I had a right to know. I feel like I've been hit by a semi.''

Throwing one last glare at George, Gabriel stalked toward the church. He needed a quiet place where he could think, could get a grip on his emotions, which were rampaging out of control. He was afraid of what he might do if he didn't get that control. With a hard shove, he pushed open one of the double doors and nearly collided with Rebecca.

"I'm sorry it took—"

"Excuse me, Rebecca.'' He hurried past her before she demanded answers he didn't have.

Stunned by Gabriel's abruptness, Rebecca watched him storm away from her. What had happened in the short time she was in the nursery? She thought about following him into the sanctuary but discarded the idea immediately. The cold look on Gabriel's face completely shut her out. He wanted her to share her emotions, but he had a hard time doing the same. Earlier she had felt hope about the direction their relationship was going. Now she wasn't so sure.

When she went outside, she knew what had sent Gabriel into the church. George McCall. She knew his face from a photograph in his file at the police station. She shouldn't have looked up the information, but her curiosity had gotten the better of her.

Rose motioned for her to come over. Rebecca covered the distance quickly, aware of a buzz of gossip.

"Did you see Gabriel?" her grandmother asked.

"Yes, briefly."

"Did he say anything? Is he going inside to clean out his locker in the choir room?"

"Clean out his locker? What do you mean?"

"Well, Bess heard him tell Samuel he couldn't remain at a church where George was."

"He went into the sanctuary. I don't know anything beyond that."

"You two are close. Go talk to him. We can't lose him."

"I got the distinct impression he wanted to be left alone." Remembering the look on his face, Rebecca shivered in the warmth of the sun.

"Nonsense. He's been left alone too long. Go to him. Be there for him. He needs someone even if he doesn't know it. You said so yourself."

But was she the person he needed? Rebecca asked herself, not for the first time.

"Shoo, child." Granny waved her toward the church.

Rebecca reluctantly headed to the church. Cautiously she inched open the door to the sanctuary and peeked in. The only light was what streamed through the stained glass windows, ribboning the hardwood floor and pews with multicolored lines as though in celebration of the Lord.

She saw Gabriel sitting in the first row with his head bent and his shoulders hunched. Her heart twisted at the sight of him, and all she wanted to do was hold him close. Her love for him propelled her into the sanctuary, the quiet click of the door echoing through the silence.

He raised his head, stiffened but didn't look around.

She proceeded toward him, her heart pounding, her pulse thundering in her ears, her loafers clacking against the floor. Slipping into the pew next to him, she waited until he spoke. His glance was sharp as it skimmed over her, leaving her in no doubt that he wasn't happy she was there. She felt the barrier between them as though it were an impregnable wall.

She gripped her hands together so tightly that her knuckles whitened. The faint aroma of lemon-scented furniture polish lingered in the air. Strips of color danced across the floor, reminding Rebecca of a kaleidoscope. And the silence ate away at her composure. But still she waited.

"You saw him?" Gabriel finally asked, his voice husky, almost a whisper.

"Yes."

"He destroyed my family and he's standing out there enjoying himself as though nothing happened while..."

The strong slope of his jaw attested to his anger. "Do you really believe that, Gabriel? Do you think he wasn't changed by what he did?"

Gabriel buried his face in his hands. Rebecca's heart wrenched. More than anything she wished she could make him whole again.

"Let it go, Gabriel. Give over your anger and guilt to God. It is destroying you—and your chance at happiness." His faith had sustained him through so much. It could help him through this trial.

"If only I had stopped the man earlier that day, my family would be alive today."

"But you didn't. You had no reason to. We all have great hindsight."

"But he intends to come back to this church, to be a constant reminder of my loss if I attend."

"You know the story of the prodigal son. This reminds me of that story Jesus told. George was lost and now he is found. Isn't that what everything is about—forgiveness and acceptance of all God's children?"

"I don't know if I can do what the Lord wants. I feel I've let Him down."

Rebecca laid her hand on Gabriel's shoulder. "Read the story in the Bible and pray for guidance. The Lord was there for you through Judy and your son's deaths. He will be there for you now. Don't do what I did."

Slanting his head to look at her, he asked, "Do you mean what you just said?"

"Of course."

"Then you have accepted God again?"

Rebecca blinked, nonplussed. "Yes," she whispered, then in a stronger voice, "yes, I have. When I look at what He has done for you, I know He was there for me. I just closed my heart to Him and wasn't listening when He spoke. Don't make the same mistake I did.''

Rebecca rose. Gabriel needed time to come to terms with his feelings. He needed time with God to work out his anger and guilt. She quietly walked away, feeling lighthearted at the prospect of the Lord being in her life again. She turned at the door and looked toward the altar. Her heart flooded with love and acceptance, feelings she hadn't experienced in a long time.

She whispered, ''Dear heavenly Father, please help Gabriel to see the way and to accept George McCall into his life. Please give him the strength to forgive himself and George. And thank you, Lord, for leading me back to You.''

For the first time in a long while she felt a complete peace. She went out into the sunshine with her head lifted toward the light.

''Three more weeks, and summer vacation will be upon us. Have you figured out what you're gonna do this summer to keep yourself busy?'' Rebecca poured Peter a glass of milk and slid the plate of home-baked cookies toward him.

''I want to work with Mrs. Wiggles and teach her some tricks.''

''How about some manners, too?''

Peter took a bite of his sugar cookie. ''I'm sorry about the shoe.''

Rebecca remembered the hole the puppy had chewed in one of her favorite navy pumps. She learned quickly to make sure closet doors were kept shut and everything of importance was off the floor. "What else do you want to do?"

"I'm gonna help Miss Bess train Peepers. I'll have more time this summer to help her. Her eyesight isn't so good, so I told her I'd read more to her. There's a baseball camp Coach told me about and there's a church camp, too." Peter gulped half his milk, and when he put the glass on the table, he had a milk mustache.

Rebecca handed him a napkin. "It looks like you've got things figured out. You do need to save some time for Josh and chores around here."

"Sure. I already told Granny I would help with Josh while you're at work. Josh and me have been practicing real hard on his exercises. He'll walk in no time."

Rebecca wished that were true. She remained quiet. She didn't want Peter to lose hope. And anything was possible where God was concerned.

When the phone rang, she said, "See if Josh is up from his afternoon nap. We need to go to Miss Bess's soon."

As Peter raced from the kitchen, Rebecca lifted the receiver, hoping it was Gabriel. He had been at church this morning but hadn't said more than two words to her. She wanted to talk to him about George's appearance at the worship service.

"Hello."

"Rebecca?"

"Yes, Craig," she said, her hands tightening on the phone.

"I'm glad I caught you. I have something I want to tell you and Peter."

Rebecca sat. "What is it?"

"I got married yesterday. Can you tell Peter for me?"

Numb, she loosened her grip on the receiver and shifted it to the other ear. "Yes, I will. Congratulations. I hope you're happy." As she said the words, she suddenly realized she meant them, and that surprised her. When had she forgiven Craig for leaving her and the boys? She knew the answer—when she had reconnected with the Lord.

"You mean it, Rebecca?"

"Yes, I do, Craig. Good luck." She hung up the phone, her hand lingering on the receiver for a few seconds while she thought about her newfound and exhilarating state of harmony.

"Mom, Josh is still asleep. Do you want me to wake him?" Peter came to a halt inside the doorway.

"Heavens, no. Never wake a sleeping child unless absolutely necessary. I suspect he didn't sleep much at the church nursery this morning. When he's around Mabel, he likes to stay up. She's so entertaining, I don't think he wants to miss anything." She removed her hand from the receiver.

"Who was that on the phone?"

"Your father."

Frowning, Peter tensed. "What did he want?"

"He got married yesterday and wanted us to know."

"I'm sorry, Mom." Peter threw his arms around Rebecca's neck and gave her a hug.

"Why are you sorry?"

Peter stepped back. "Doesn't it make you sad he's remarrying?"

Cocking her head, Rebecca replied, "You know, Peter, it doesn't. I'm glad he's found someone to make him happy." As she spoke, there was a part of her that was amazed by her words. But she meant them, and that surprised her even more. "How do you feel about it?"

Peter shrugged. "Kinda the same way. I wish Dad was around more, but even when we lived in Dallas, he wasn't, very much. I'm just not the kind of son he wants."

"That's not true," she said automatically, not wanting her son to feel that way.

"I never could please him. I tried. I just couldn't."

The sadness in her son's voice tore at her. She pulled him to her and held him close, fighting the tears threatening to flow. "You know, son, that's your father's problem, not yours. He expects people to be perfect, and we aren't."

"Coach has told me the only way we really learn is by our mistakes."

"Well, I know one thing, young man. You're the son I want. I'm lucky to have you and Josh." Her arms tightened about him.

"Mom! I can't breathe."

Chuckling, she released her hold on Peter, and he quickly backed away. "Sorry. I got carried away. Moms do that from time to time."

"Just don't let the guys see you. I'd never live it down."

"I'll remember that. Seriously, Peter, are you okay?"

"Sure. Look at all the people who care about me. There's Granny, Miss Bess and Coach. And I have lots of friends now at school and church. I'm lucky."

Even though her son's words were said in a cheerful tone, she knew underlying them the sadness still lingered. His eyes lacked a bright sparkle, and there was a slight slump to his posture. His sorrow wouldn't go away overnight, if ever, but she realized living in Oakview would help Peter forget his father's indifference. The good people of Oakview weren't indifferent to anything, and she was beginning to appreciate the small town, where everybody knew everything about everybody else.

Glancing at her watch, Rebecca frowned. "You know, Peter, Josh has been down longer than usual. He's been fighting a cold for the past few days. I'd better check on him."

"Remember not to wake him," Peter called as she made her way up the stairs to her bedroom.

Peering into the crib, she half expected to see Josh with his eyes open, amusing himself by watching his brightly colored fish mobile. She saw neither. He was still asleep. Something was wrong. His breathing was wrong. His color was pale. She shook him.

Alarm bolted through her. She couldn't wake him up. Snatching him, she held his limp form in her arms. Panic took hold.

"Peter," she shouted, placing Josh on the floor and tilting his head back to open his airway. "Call nine-one-one."

Peter came running. "Mom, what's wrong?"

She checked Josh's pulse in his neck. "Call nine-one-one," she repeated as the steps of the lifesaving procedure clicked through her mind.

When Rebecca breathed into Josh's mouth, she noticed his chest didn't rise. Her hot air blasted her face. Blocked airway. Quickly she pressed with one hand on his stomach several times, then she began breathing for him, praying as she had never prayed before. *Please, dear God, don't take Josh. Please, please save my son.*

After several breaths Josh started screaming, and relief trembled through Rebecca. *Thank you, heavenly Father.*

Chapter Twelve

Rebecca paced from one end of the waiting room to the other, every few seconds checking the doorway for the emergency room nurse. Her heartbeat pulsated in her ears with each quick step she took. The antiseptic smells she associated with hospitals made her stomach churn. The sound of upbeat music over the intercom system grated on her nerves. The glare of the bright fluorescent lights gave her a headache.

Memories of other times she had spent in an emergency room waiting for a report on her youngest son flooded her mind, heightening her sense of aloneness. She glanced toward the doorway and stopped in her tracks. Gabriel stood there, his expression filled with anguish. She took one look at his face and rushed into his embrace.

"What's wrong with Josh, Rebecca?" Gabriel's hand stroked her back, his touch soothing, his voice caressing her soul.

"He wasn't breathing. I did CPR and he started breathing again, but I was so scared. The doctor is checking him over right now." She leaned back to look into his face. "How did you find out so fast?"

"Mabel heard Peter's call. She radioed me. What can I do to help you?"

Those words, never spoken by her ex-husband, underscored how different everything was in Oakview. You can help me by never letting me go, she thought.

She drew in a deep, fortifying breath, refusing to waste another second dreaming of what would never be. "Granny doesn't drive after dark. Could you bring her and Peter to the hospital? I imagine by now they are beside themselves. I told them as I was leaving with the ambulance that I would call when I talked with the doctor, but I know Granny. She would rather be here waiting than at home."

"Of course, I'll get them. Anything else?"

"Hold me." The words came out without her thinking about what they might imply. She desperately needed to feel a spiritual and physical connection to someone at the moment. That feeling of being alone that she had gotten often in Dallas had inundated her while she had fought to give Josh his next breath and on the short ride to the hospital. She needed to wipe it away before it consumed her again.

His arms about her tightened, and she laid her head on his chest, listening to the strong beat of his heart, its steady rhythm a balm. When she was in his embrace, she felt anchored. She cherished the feeling for a few precious moments before she pulled away.

"Thank you." She viewed him through a shimmer of tears.

He framed her face. "You aren't alone, Rebecca. I'm here for you. God's here for you. I won't be gone long. I'll bring Peter and Rose back."

She watched him leave, and a feeling of bereavement descended as though a part of her had left. The tears pooling in her eyes spilled down her cheeks, and she wiped them away. When she finally did get to see him, Josh mustn't sense her distress. She had to be strong for him and Peter.

She walked to the picture window and followed Gabriel's progress across the parking lot to his Jeep. She had a few minutes before her family would be here. She made a decision.

She hurried into the hall, then asked the lady at the reception desk, "Where's the chapel?"

The woman gestured with her right hand. "Down that way, third door on the left."

"If anyone is looking for Rebecca Michaels, that's where I'll be."

Rebecca followed the receptionist's directions and went inside. The small room had two rows of pews and an altar bearing a simple wooden cross. The grating canned music in the waiting room was refreshingly absent. The bright lights were gone, replaced with soft illumination that offered a tranquil dimness. Here, in the Lord's house, peace prevailed over chaos, filling Rebecca with a quiet strength. She'd come to the right place. The Lord would know what to do.

Sitting on the first row, she clasped her hands in

front of her and bowed her head. "Please, Lord, forgive me for turning away from you. I now know I was wrong. Please help me to find the strength to weather this latest crisis and show me the way back into Your arms. You have given me so much, and for a time I had forgotten that. Josh is just a baby. Please don't make him suffer for my mistakes."

Rebecca stayed for a few minutes, letting her mind go blank while she absorbed the serenity of her surroundings. When she stood, she felt whole and no longer alone. God was with her as she walked from the chapel to find her family. He would be with her through this crisis.

Gabriel escorted Granny and Peter through the double doors. Rebecca's son spotted her and ran to her, throwing his arms around her waist. He buried his face against her body and squeezed tightly.

"Josh will be fine, Peter. God will take care of him." She caressed her eldest son's hair.

Granny leaned heavily on her cane with each weary step, concern in her expression. "Have they told you anything yet?"

"No, but it shouldn't be too much longer."

As they started for the waiting room, a doctor came toward Rebecca. She paused, clasping Peter's shoulder.

"Mrs. Michaels, Josh will be all right. I want to keep him overnight, and if he's okay tomorrow, he can go home then. He has bronchitis. I'll give you some medicine for him. You can go in now and see him before we transfer him to a regular room."

"Can I see Josh, too?" Peter asked.

"Sure. Don't stay long. I want to get him settled into a room soon," the doctor answered, indicating the way.

When Rebecca entered the room, followed by her family and Gabriel, a woman turned from the bed and said, "I'm the respiratory therapist. I just gave him a breathing treatment. He's hooked up to a pulse ox machine to measure the oxygen saturation of his body. That's what this is." She showed them Josh's finger, which looked like it had a Band-Aid on it. "And he has an IV."

Rebecca thanked the therapist, glad for the explanation. Josh looked so small in the hospital bed with tubes in him and a mask on his face. His eyes were closed.

"He's sleeping now. He's had quite a night, as I'm sure you all have," the therapist said.

Rebecca took Josh's free hand and held it for a moment while Peter stood next to her. Granny and Gabriel moved to the other side of the bed. Rebecca said a prayer of thanks, then released Josh. She motioned for everyone to leave. Granny bent and kissed Josh's forehead, then she walked to the door. Gabriel whispered something into Josh's ear and followed Granny out of the room.

Peter remained by the bed. "Josh, wait until you get home. You won't believe how much Mrs. Wiggles is getting into everything. She ate one of your favorite toys, which I promise to replace." His voice grew thick. "It fell out of your bed—she found it on the floor."

Standing behind him, Rebecca placed both hands

on Peter's shoulders. "This looks worse than it is. You heard what the therapist and the doctor said. He will be fine."

"It isn't fair that bad things keep happening to him." Peter whirled and pressed himself against Rebecca, his arms clinging to her. The sound of her son crying ripped through her, momentarily making her feel helpless. Then she remembered how much the Lord loved them all, and she found the strength to deal with her son's anguish.

She sat in the chair next to the bed and clasped her son's upper arms. "Honey, bad things happen to everyone. Just as good things do, too. What's important is how we handle those things. Josh is a trooper. That makes him even more special than he already is. I think he's pretty lucky. He has you as a brother."

Peter sniffed. "You think?"

"I wouldn't have said it if I didn't. I told you once I wouldn't lie to you, and that won't change."

"Are you still mad at God?"

"No, honey. I was wrong to be angry at God for what happened to me. I didn't handle things very well, but that will change. I have learned from my mistake."

Peter hugged her. "Mom, I love you."

"I love you, honey. Now let's get out of here so they can move Josh to a regular room and we all can get some sleep tonight."

"Are you gonna stay with Josh?"

"Yeah. I'm going to have them set up a cot in his room so I can be there when he wakes up."

"Can I stay the night with you two?" Peter asked while they walked into the hall, where Granny and Gabriel were standing.

"You've got school tomorrow. I'll call you in the morning and let you know how the night went with Josh before you go to school." Rebecca caught Gabriel's intense gaze on her. "Would you please take them home?"

He nodded.

Gabriel hung back while Peter and Granny headed for the double doors that led outside. "Are you okay?" His touch whisper soft, he grazed her cheek with the pad of his thumb.

She smiled, warmed by his presence more than she cared to acknowledge. "Yes." She clasped his hand. "Thank you for taking care of Granny and Peter for me."

"I told you you weren't alone."

"I know that now."

He bent and gave her a quick kiss that left her stunned. Sunlight flooded her system. Angels sang. It had only been a peck, but sensations deep inside made her toes curl. She couldn't imagine what would happen if he really kissed her.

Rebecca rested her head on the back of the cushioned chair and stared unseeingly at the ceiling in Josh's hospital room. She listened to the quiet reigning on the floor and relaxed.

The sound of the door opening brought her up in her chair, and she twisted to see who was coming into the room. Gabriel entered, and her heart soared.

He offered her a tender smile that had the ability to dissolve her apprehension. She remained where she was. She was afraid if she tried to stand she would collapse from exhaustion.

"You didn't have to come back."

"I know, but I wanted to see how Josh was doing—and how you were doing."

"We're both fine."

Gabriel covered the distance to the bed and stared at Josh, who was lost-looking in the white sheets. Myriad emotions—from worry to relief to joy—flittered across Gabriel's face, each one making Rebecca's pulse race. There were few people who cared and loved her son as the man before her was showing in the tender glow of his eyes.

"When Mabel called to tell me that Josh was being rushed to the hospital, I thought—" He shook his head. "I thought I might lose him."

Rebecca rose and placed her hand on his shoulder to comfort him. "As you can see, he will be all right."

He pivoted toward her, clasping her hands. "Rebecca, I want to take care of you and your sons."

Her heart stopped beating for a second, then began to pound a mad staccato against her chest. Her palms became sweaty, and her throat went dry.

"I would be a good father and husband to you, Josh and Peter."

She opened her mouth to reply, but no words came out. Her mind went blank. Her body trembled.

"Say something. Anything."

She moved back, needing to sit down before she collapsed. "I don't know what to say."

He took two steps and drew her against him. "Think about it, at least. I would never abandon you or your sons. Never."

His mouth came down upon hers, and his kiss robbed her of any rational thought and stole her breath. She felt cherished and capable of floating on a cloud high above the earth. His arms wound about her while his possession deepened to claim her. Her length meshed into his as though they were one.

When he moved back and looked at her, she thought she was dreaming, that somehow she had fallen asleep and would awaken at any moment. He cupped her face and started to kiss her again.

But Rebecca felt the coldness of his ring against her cheek and sobered to the situation. She pulled back. "Why do you want to take care of us? What does that mean?"

"I want to marry you. When I thought I might lose Josh, I went a little crazy. It made me realize I might have run out of time. Your boys need a father to love them."

"I agree, and I need a husband to love me. Is that what you're saying?"

"I love you, Rebecca."

"Then why do you still have your ring on?"

"I forgot—no, that's not quite right." He backed away, combing his hand through his hair. "I don't know why. I know I have deep feelings for you. I want us to be a family. That was made clear to me tonight."

She stood straight, as though a rod had been placed down her back. "Maybe until you forgive yourself and George, you feel you need to wear that ring as a symbol of what you imagine is your sin, like in *The Scarlet Letter*. I don't see us having a future until you deal with your past. My son is fine. There is no hurry." She sank onto the chair, desperately trying to hold herself together. "Good night, Gabriel. I won't be in to work tomorrow."

When the quiet swish of the door indicated he had left the room, Rebecca finally showed her emotion. She felt her face crumple, her body sink in on itself. He had kissed her like a man who had believed in a future, but he still wore a part of his past like a brand. He had helped her through her problems. Why couldn't she help him through his?

Rebecca stared at Gabriel's house.

Only one light shone in the living room window. And somehow that one light symbolized the loneliness in her heart. Was Gabriel lonely, too?

She shouldn't be surprised that she'd gone for a walk and ended up at his place. He'd been on her mind all day. She'd managed to avoid talking to him on the phone because she would have felt awkward after the night before when he had asked her to marry him.

But they needed to talk.

She couldn't go on like this. While spending the day at the hospital with Josh, she'd had a great deal of time to think.

She was so tempted to accept Gabriel's proposal

and hope that he would resolve his problems concerning his wife and child's untimely deaths. But what if that never happened? What if all he really felt for Rebecca was compassion and pity? She couldn't—wouldn't—base a marriage on that, no matter how much the man loved her children, and there was no doubt he loved them very much.

Squaring her shoulders, she marched up the steps and rang the bell. A few minutes later Gabriel swung the door open, his tired, grim expression dissolving when he saw her. His weak smile tilted her world while steeling her resolve. She wanted all of him— not only his breathtaking smile but his heart.

"Rebecca."

Had she ever heard her name said so sweetly? The sound on his lips coaxed her to forget what was at stake. That would be the biggest mistake, because she would be settling for less than she wanted, deserved.

"I thought you were George McCall."

"Why?"

"He called me at the station. He wanted to see me. I told him I was leaving to go home and didn't want to see him."

Her heart wrenched. George would be a constant reminder of the past to Gabriel until he dealt with the man.

"Please, come in. I just got home. It's been a long day. I was going to come by, but I wanted to change out of my uniform first and grab something to eat. How's Josh doing since you brought him home this afternoon?"

"Fine. The medicine is helping, and his breathing seems to be okay. I have a monitor on him when I'm not in the room. He's sleeping right now, and Granny is listening for any signs of trouble." Rebecca patted the pocket of her jeans. "I have my cell phone if there's a problem. I just needed to get out and get some fresh air. I started walking and ended up here." She listened to herself chatter a mile a minute and realized she was nervous. She had never confronted a man about loving her—not even Craig.

"Would you like something to drink or to eat?" Gabriel led the way into the kitchen. "I was just about to warm up something for dinner."

She shook her head. "Granny had a feast for me when I came home from the hospital with Josh. She declared I probably lost at least a few pounds from not eating, so she was determined to make sure I made up for it all in one meal."

"Did you?"

"Nope. I've lost my appetite."

"Why?"

She looked him directly in the eye. "My stomach is tied up in knots."

"Why?"

"Because all I thought about today was your proposal."

He arched a brow. "And?"

"And nothing. I don't know what to do anymore."

He closed the space between them but didn't touch her. She was glad, because that would have totally unraveled her. As it was, her composure was held together by a thin thread. His commanding presence was doing enough to her nervous system. She had never been so drawn to a man and yet so afraid to act on that attraction.

"Rebecca, I didn't mean to make matters worse for you. I want to help."

"Why?"

"Because I care for you."

"That's not enough, Gabriel. I'll never settle for less than all of a person ever again. Can you truthfully say you can give me that?"

He fingered his ring, twisting it. Then he yanked it off. "There. Is that what you want? I should have done that a long time ago."

Her shoulders sagged as though a great weight were pushing her down. Indeed, all she wanted to do was sink into the floor. "I want you to mean it. I can tell by the expression in your eyes you haven't yet made peace with yourself."

He clenched the ring. The cold metal dug into his flesh, painfully reminding him of the cold past he couldn't forget. "What do I have to do to prove my love to you?"

"I—"

The sound of the doorbell cut into tension-fraught air. Gabriel growled his frustration and went to answer the bell. Rebecca followed, intending to escape before she fell apart in front of him. His finger might be ringless, but his heart was still burdened.

Gabriel wrenched the door open and froze. George looked from Gabriel to Rebecca then back to Gabriel, determination in his eyes. Gabriel gripped the edge of the door and fought the urge to slam it in George's face.

"I told you I didn't want to talk," Gabriel said, his body taut.

"I think we need to."

"I have nothing to say."

"But I have something to say to you. May I come in?"

"No."

Rebecca laid a hand on his arm. "Gabriel, I think you should listen to what the man has to say."

He glared at her, shaking off her touch. "You do?" He heard the sarcastic edge to his voice but didn't care. He was tired of people telling him what to do where George McCall was concerned. He could wallow in self-pity if he chose to. It was no one else's business.

"Please, Gabriel."

The pain reflected in her gaze tore at the barrier he had built around his heart. He could see in her eyes that he had shut her out again and that there could be no future for them until he could open his heart totally to her. One brick fell, then another. "For you."

"No, Gabriel, for yourself," she murmured, and left him alone with George.

With Rebecca's every step down the stone path, Gabriel felt abandoned. Why had she left him alone with his tormentor? It was easier not to face the past, to bury it deeply and not deal with the pain. Gritting his teeth, Gabriel slowly pivoted toward George, drilling his glare into the man.

Yet in the face of Gabriel's anger, George's expression softened with understanding. "Believe me, I know there's nothing I can say that will bring your family back. I'll pay for that the rest of my life."

"You came all the way over here to tell me that?"

"One of the things I promised myself in prison was that I would seek you out and apologize—no matter how difficult it was. I am so sorry for what I did. I replay that afternoon in my mind every day."

"So do I," Gabriel said, then realized that wasn't true anymore. Ever since Rebecca had entered his life, he had thought less and less about the day of the accident.

"I hope one day you can forgive me. I've made my peace with God, but it's important that I try to make my peace with you, too. All I can say is that I'll spend the rest of my life trying to make up for that mistake."

"Why did you come back to Oakview?"

"This is my home. The only people I know live here. I have a problem that I'm coping with, but I need people who care around me. I'm not as strong as you."

His statement slammed into Gabriel, humbling him. If he was as strong as George thought, he should be able to forgive the man and move on with his life, open his heart totally to another—someone who deserved only the best. The sadness he'd seen in Rebecca's expression added salt to his open wound. It festered and bled.

"I came here today to beg you not to leave our church. I need their support, but you're an intricate part of that congregation. Your loss would be felt by so many, and I don't know if I could handle that on top of putting my life back together.''

''Who said I was going to leave?'' Gabriel asked, surprised by the man's plea.

George shrugged. ''You know the rumor mill in our town.''

Our town. Those words made Gabriel realize he didn't own Oakview. Nor did he have a say on who lived there. ''Yes, but I never said that. I don't know if I could give up the support of my church, either.''

''Then you understand what I'm saying.''

''Yes,'' Gabriel reluctantly admitted, hating the fact he did know how George felt. That realization took him one step closer to forgiving the man.

George strode toward the front door, pausing before opening it. ''Please think about what I said. I'll try to stay out of your way as much as possible. I don't want to make this any harder on you.''

The click of the door closing echoed through the empty house. Gabriel gripped the back of the chair until the tips of his fingers whitened. Exhaustion weaved its way down his length. In a split second three years before so many lives had been changed. Until this moment, however, he hadn't thought of George's life being altered. He had only thought of himself. Gabriel sank onto the wing chair, resting his head on the cushion, his eyes closed.

Thoughts swirled in his mind, making a jumbled mess. But from the chaos came the picture of Rebecca smiling at him, touching his arm, connecting with him on a level beyond friendship. She needed him; he needed her.

His eyes snapped open. She was right. If he didn't deal with his past, there could be no real future with her and her sons. His hatred would fester until it consumed him, defining his life.

Gabriel saw his Bible on the table next to him and picked it up. Remembering what Rebecca had said to him in the church a few days before, he flipped through the pages until he came to the story about the prodigal son. He read it, absorbing each word, taking it into his mind and delving beneath the words to seek the true meaning. It was a story of forgiveness, of giving a person a second chance.

"And he said unto him, Son, thou art ever with me, and all that I have is thine. It was meet that we should make merry, and be glad for this thy brother was dead, and is alive again; and was lost, and is found." Gabriel read the parable from St. Luke 15:31. Could he welcome George into the church and forgive him for what he had done against Gabriel?

He closed his Bible and prayed for the guidance he needed to rid his mind and soul of the anger that threatened to destroy him. As he said the Lord's Prayer, he felt a tranquillity wash over him, cleansing him of his rage. A balance was restored.

He drew his wedding ring from his pocket, rose and went to his bedroom. He opened a keepsake box, put the piece of his past inside, then closed it. God had taken Judy from him, but in His wisdom, He had given him Rebecca. Now, all he had to do was convince Rebecca that he loved her as well as her children.

Chapter Thirteen

Rebecca hated calling in sick for a second day in a row, but she wanted to make sure Josh was all right before leaving him while she worked. She chuckled when she hung up from talking with Mabel. She had to convince the woman not to come over and help her with Josh. Their relationship had come a long way in the few months she had worked at the police station. Gabriel had been right about Mabel being a softie.

Gabriel had been right about a lot of things. When Josh had been in the hospital, she hadn't turned away from God but had grown closer to Him. She felt whole again, as though a part of her wasn't floating around unattached.

Gabriel and the people of Oakview had shown her the way back to the Lord. Why couldn't she help Gabriel deal with his past? If they were to have a meaningful relationship, he would have to open his heart to her support.

Her heart ached when she thought about the scene at Gabriel's house the evening before with George. Gabriel had closed off an important part of himself. Not being able to forgive George had fueled Gabriel's anger, his ties to his past. Memories were important but not when they dominated a person's life and kept him from truly opening himself up to another.

The sound of the doorbell startled Rebecca. She hoped Mabel hadn't ignored what she had said and come anyway. She felt bad enough not going in to work without the whole office staff being gone. And knowing Mabel, she probably had ignored her.

As Rebecca threw open the door, she opened her mouth to tell Mabel to go back to work, but the words died in her throat. Craig, a beautiful woman dressed in a neat pair of slacks and a silk blouse, and two children stood on her front porch. My ex-husband's new family, she thought.

Rebecca forced a smile to her lips. "I wasn't expecting you, Craig." Her tight hold on the doorknob made her hand ache, but she didn't release her grip.

He tried to smile but failed. "I know I should have said something on the phone Sunday, but I wasn't sure I would accept the job."

"What job?" Apprehension washed over her. She wasn't going to like what Craig had to say.

"I'm starting a new job at a bank in New York City in two weeks. We're moving and decided not to wait once I made the decision to take the job." Craig gestured toward his car, which was packed full.

"That's awfully fast." She strongly suspected it

had been a fact when she had talked with him a few days before, but she didn't have the energy to call him on it. Frankly, she found it didn't matter except that the boys would be farther away from their father. Of course, if he didn't want to see them five or five hundred miles wouldn't matter.

"I thought I would stop by and say goodbye to Peter."

"How about Josh? Peter's at school." Surprisingly the slight to her youngest son didn't arouse her anger. If Craig chose not to be in his two sons' lives, then that was his loss.

"Josh, too. When's Peter coming home?" He peered at his watch, his face pinched into a frown.

"He should be here in an hour. Since Josh has been sick, Peter wants to make sure he's okay and has been coming home for lunch."

Craig looked at his new wife, and she nodded. "Then we'll wait for him to come home. We can't stay long since I want to make St. Louis tonight."

His response didn't surprise Rebecca. He had never cared to ask about Josh when they had lived together. But the fact he again showed how he really felt hurt. "That's a long drive. Are you sure you should wait?"

"Yes," he said on a long sigh.

"Then come in and wait in the living room." Rebecca swung the door wide and waited until the family filed into the house before following them inside.

"I'm Rebecca Michaels," she said to the beautiful woman with long auburn hair and a face perfectly made up to enhance her two best features, her blue eyes and high cheekbones. Rebecca noted that after several hours in the car the woman's blouse was still tucked into her neatly pressed slacks. Looking at her jeans and T-shirt, Rebecca inwardly groaned.

"I'm Laura Michaels, and these are my two daughters, Mandy and Sara."

Hearing the woman say Craig's surname reminded Rebecca of her failure to keep her marriage together and shook her self-confidence, which she had worked so hard to rebuild. "It's nice meeting you. Please have a seat."

Rebecca greeted each of the little girls who appeared to be six and eight years old. They were perfect little replicas of their mother, with long auburn hair brushed back from their pretty faces. They wore matching dresses with few wrinkles, the soft burgundy fabric complementing their creamy, smooth complexions.

Mandy and Sara quietly sat on the couch, their backs straight, their hands folded in their laps. Rebecca thought of Peter, who couldn't sit on a couch for more than a minute before he started to wiggle or talk. Or Josh, who until very recently couldn't sit up by himself. Far from perfect, but they were her sons, and she loved them dearly.

"May I get you something to drink?" Rebecca started for the kitchen, needing something to do while they waited for Peter.

"No, we're fine," Craig said, stopping her in her tracks.

Rebecca turned and glanced at the clock on the mantel, its ticking filling the quiet. Slowly she walked to a chair and sat. While she searched her mind for a topic of conversation, she listened to the ticking of the clock. What would the couple across from her do if she ran from the room screaming? She decided she wasn't much better than Peter at sitting still and being quiet.

"Oakview hasn't changed, I see," Craig finally said.

"I like the fact it hasn't." Rebecca winced at her defensive tone. Craig had always hated coming to see Granny, and when they had come to visit, he had made sure they hadn't stayed long.

"What do you do for fun around here?"

"It isn't that small. There's a movie theater with first-run movies. The town is big on sports, and there is great fishing in some of the streams and rivers nearby."

Another lengthy silence tautened Rebecca's nerves until she thought they would snap and she would go running from the room screaming. The doorbell sounded, cutting into the tension. She leaped to her feet and ran to the door, opening it without even looking to see who it was. It didn't matter. Anyone was better than her present guests.

Gabriel greeted her with a smile.

She returned his smile and sagged against the door, relieved to see a friendly face. The tired lines about his mouth and eyes drew her attention. She wanted to smooth them away, to ask how the night before with George went. She held onto the door to keep from reaching out to him. This wasn't the time to discuss George or their relationship.

"Am I glad to see you!" Rebecca exclaimed in a voice barely audible.

"You are?"

"Yes, of course."

"I thought after last night you wouldn't be."

"Craig and his new wife and family are here," she whispered, nodding toward the living room.

"We need to talk. How long is he going to be here?"

The venom behind the word *he* was clear to Rebecca. She relished the protective ring to his voice. "Too long. Until Peter comes home for lunch, which is in—" she glanced at her watch "—thirty minutes. What do you want to talk about?"

"It will have to wait."

"Please come in." She tried to keep from sounding desperate, but she needed moral support.

"I don't think I should. I might not be very nice to him."

Rebecca grabbed Gabriel's hand. "Sure you can." She tugged him into her house and closed the door before he changed his mind and escaped.

When she entered the living room, she introduced Gabriel to Craig and his new family. "Gabriel, our town's police chief, is my boss since I started working at the police station."

"Who takes care of the boys?" Craig asked after shaking hands with Gabriel.

Since when have you cared? That was what Rebecca wanted to say, but she forced herself to count to ten before answering, "Granny takes care of them."

"Do you think your grandmother should take care of Peter and Josh? That seems like an awfully lot of work for an old woman."

"This *old* woman can handle it just fine. Not that you've ever cared if I lived or died." Granny came into the room with Josh in her arms. "I heard you down here and thought you might like to say hello to your son." Granny thrust Josh into Craig's lap, then moved to sit in her rocking chair.

Craig clasped Josh before he toppled over and held him gingerly, as though he didn't know what to do with the child. He surged to his feet, gripping Josh under the arms and holding him away from his body. Quickly Craig covered the distance to Rebecca and gave Josh to her.

"I think he needs changing." Craig's nose wrinkled, a frown marring his features.

Rebecca seized the chance to escape the room, knowing that Granny would have changed him before coming downstairs. "I'll be back in a moment."

"I'll help you," Gabriel added, trailing behind Rebecca.

Upstairs in her bedroom, she laid Josh on her bed and checked to see if she needed to change his diaper. She didn't. She felt Gabriel's gaze on her as she buttoned Josh's pants. Suddenly she was all thumbs.

"When did Craig get married again?"

"I just found out about it right before Josh was rushed to the hospital."

"How do you feel about this?"

"Craig's getting what he wants, his perfect little family."

"You didn't answer my question."

"I'm sad that he's turning his back on his sons, but beyond that I don't feel anything. I refuse to waste any more energy trying to change something I can't change."

"No anger?"

She shook her head. "I guess I'm mellowing. How about you?" she asked in a casual tone. Inside she was anything but casual. She held her breath while waiting for his reply.

"I'm mellowing, too. Must be catching."

She noticed his wedding ring was still off his left hand, but she wasn't going to say anything about it. Seeing Craig with his new family didn't arouse her anger, but it did make her leery about any relationship a person wasn't committed to one hundred percent. She had to protect her heart and her children from being hurt again.

"I guess I've stalled changing Josh's diaper long enough. I probably shouldn't have left Craig with Granny. They never got along before, and now he definitely isn't on her favorite people list."

"Here, let me." Gabriel took Josh and swung him high.

The sound of her son's laughter dissolved some of her anxiety. Josh had a way of putting her life in perspective, of teaching her what was important. And having Gabriel hold her youngest gave her a sense of satisfaction. She knew he was trying in his own way to make a point with Craig, but she wasn't sure her ex-husband would get it.

When Rebecca entered the living room, the tension hit her like a brick wall. She looked from Granny to Craig then back to Granny. Her grandmother smiled so sweetly Rebecca knew she'd had her say while Rebecca was gone and Craig wasn't too pleased by it.

Craig stood, throwing her grandmother a narrow eyed look. "I think we'll wait outside by the car."

"Well, if you're sure that's what you want to do. Peter will be here in a few minutes."

Craig, with family in tow, stalked to the front door.

Rebecca peered at Granny, who shrugged and appeared innocent. "They're our guests."

"I didn't invite him here. Did you?"

"No, but he wanted to see Peter. I'll never deny him that."

Granny huffed. "It seems to me there are people in this town who are better fathers to that boy than his own." After looking pointedly at Gabriel, she headed toward the kitchen.

"No one can accuse my grandmother of being subtle. I'm sorry, Gabriel." She avoided his gaze, afraid of what might be in his eyes.

"She's right. I want to be a father to Peter and Josh."

Rebecca wasn't sure he was aware of the pain that laced his words. She knew he wanted to be a father, but at what cost? "I'd better get outside for when Peter comes home. I don't want him hurt any more than necessary." She started for the front door.

"Rebecca, I put my wedding ring away for good."

She stopped, her hand on the door, her back to Gabriel.

"I'm working on forgiving George. I wish I could say I have completely. I've lived with this anger and guilt for a long time, but with God's help I will forgive."

Her grip tightened. "Gabriel, I can't deal with this right now. I don't know how Peter will react when he sees his father and his new family."

"My proposal still stands. I want to marry you."

She shivered. Suddenly she was so cold. She pivoted at the door and faced Gabriel, who was still holding Josh. "Me or my children?"

"You. I love your children, but you're the woman I want to marry."

"I can't answer you right now." She pulled the door open.

"I think you're the one who is afraid, Rebecca. You're scared of being hurt again. It's easier to make it seem like my problems are what is keeping us apart. It's easier for you to shut off your feelings than to risk getting hurt again."

She quirked one of her brows. "Oh, and you didn't shut off your feelings? So now you're the expert on relationships?"

Gabriel watched Rebecca flee outside. He shook his head. "I don't know, Josh, about your mother. Have any suggestions on how I can reach her?"

"I do."

Gabriel turned toward Rose, who stood in the entrance to the living room, using her cane to support her. These past few days had been difficult on Rose—on everyone.

"Don't take no for an answer, son."

''That's all?''

''Craig's just stirred up some feelings she's been having a tough time dealing with. She'll come around after he leaves.''

''She demanded I come to terms with my problems, and I have. But she still hasn't completely faced hers.''

''Give her some time. She will. You're a mighty powerful persuader.'' Granny walked to the front door and started to close it. ''Come on into the kitchen, and we'll talk over some coffee.''

Rebecca heard the sound of the front door closing behind her and almost hurried to push it open and escape inside where she was accepted for who she was. Instead, she gripped the porch railing and observed Craig and his family standing by the car. Craig's arms were folded over his chest, and his thunderous expression slashed his eyebrows and mouth downward. The three females remained quietly lined up next to him. In that moment she pitied Laura.

When Peter came running down the sidewalk, Rebecca straightened, praying that Craig would let their son down gently.

Peter stopped short when he saw Craig. Rebecca listened to Craig introduce Peter to his wife and her two daughters. There was a note of pride in Craig's voice that made her grip the railing tightly. *Lord, please give me the strength to handle this, to be there for Peter after his father leaves.*

She didn't have to hear the conversation to know exactly when Craig informed Peter he was moving to New York. Her son frowned, his teeth digging into his bottom lip. He had been okay with his father remarrying, but this was different. She wanted to go to her son and hug him, but she knew her presence would only compound the situation with Craig. Ten minutes later, Craig patted Peter on the head and told him goodbye, that he would call him soon.

As Craig climbed into the car, Rebecca descended the steps and walked to her son. Placing her hands on his shoulders, she squeezed and whispered, "I love you."

Craig's car disappeared from view before Peter said, "I know, Mom, but why can't Dad love me, too?"

She turned her son to face her. "He does love you, honey. If he didn't, he wouldn't have come by and told you personally about him moving. Some people have a hard time showing their love. Your dad is one of those people, but it doesn't mean he doesn't love you." She pulled him toward the steps and sat. "You should have seen the first time he saw you and held you. The look of wonder on his face was priceless."

"Really?"

"Yes. You were a beautiful baby."

"Mom! Boys aren't beautiful."

"Sorry, I meant handsome. And remember the time you learned to ride your bicycle? He was there helping you."

"But he has a new family now."

"People are capable of loving more than one person. He'll have room in his heart for all of you."

She prayed that was true, but if it wasn't, she would be there to pick up the pieces.

Her son's stomach rumbled. He laughed. "I guess I'm hungry. We worked hard this morning at school."

"And you need to get back. Let's see what Granny cooked for lunch."

They mounted the steps to the porch. Rebecca was aware that Gabriel was still inside with her grandmother. She didn't want to see him right now. Craig's surprise visit left her feeling vulnerable, wounded, and she needed time to sort through the emotions swirling inside her.

"I bet Granny fixed ham and cheese sandwiches with tomato soup."

"You think?"

"It's Tuesday. She does every Tuesday for the lunch I take to school."

In the kitchen Gabriel sat at the table, cradling a cup of coffee while he spoke with her grandmother. He fell silent when she and Peter entered the room. A blush stained her cheeks. She obviously had been the topic of conversation. If she hadn't been so preoccupied with Peter the past few minutes, her ears would have no doubt been burning.

Gabriel pushed to his feet. "I need to get back to the station. I've played hooky too long. I'm afraid Mabel might come and hunt me down. Walk me to the door, Rebecca."

Reluctantly she led the way. When she reached out to open the door, Gabriel grasped her hand. The touch nearly sent her into his arms. Then she remembered Craig's visit and stepped back, their fingers still laced together.

"I know today hasn't been easy for you, Rebecca, but I'm not leaving without at least telling you I love you and doing this." Gabriel tugged her flat against him, and his mouth descended to claim hers.

Tingling sensations rocked her resolve to keep her distance, to wade through the emotions she was feeling. She gripped his shoulders to keep herself upright. Her legs felt like rubber and her heart felt on fire.

"Remember that. I'll see you tonight. You and I need to have a long talk and work all this out."

Gabriel left her standing in the middle of the entrance with her quivering fingers grazing the lips he had kissed so thoroughly. *I love you.* His words sang loud and clear in her mind, declaring his intentions.

Dare she take another chance on love? Rebecca wondered as she finished putting the last dinner plate in the dishwasher. She had been wrong once and was still paying dearly for it.

"Rebecca?"

She hadn't heard him enter the kitchen. Slowly she turned to face Gabriel who stood across the room— too far away yet too close. She felt as though she teetered on the brink of something important.

He strode toward her, determination in his gaze. To coat her suddenly dry throat, she swallowed several times, but she didn't move an inch. She felt trapped by his possessive look, which skimmed down her, laying claim to her.

"I'd hoped to be here earlier, but Susan reported Bess missing."

"She did? Why didn't you call me? Where is Bess? Can I help?"

Holding up his hand, close to her mouth but not touching her, he chuckled. "Bess is fine. She was asleep in someone else's room. Thought it was hers and took a nap."

Relieved, Rebecca eased back against the counter, aware of his nearness, which caused a fluttering in the pit of her stomach and siphoned the energy from her legs. "There are days I forget she has trouble with her memory from time to time, then something like that happens."

"We found her when Peepers wanted out of the room and began to yelp."

"She wasn't supposed to have the puppy inside during the day. Why am I surprised she did?"

"Bess isn't one for the rules. Everything's okay now. I even got Susan to overlook the puppy being inside."

With each moment he stood in her kitchen, her heart beat a shade faster until she was afraid she would become light-headed. She needed to put some distance between them. She ran her hand through her hair, then gestured toward the table. "Do you want something to eat? I could fix you a plate."

"There's only one thing I want."

"What do you want?" she asked, her voice a weak thread, her throat constricting.

"I want you to be my wife." He captured her face between his hands and stared into her eyes. "You're the one I love above everyone else. Yes, I love your sons, but it's you I'm asking to marry me. I want to make that perfectly clear right up front."

"I don't—"

He stopped her words with a fingertip pressed against her lips. "I am *not* Craig. Give me a chance to prove that. I know you're wary of committing to someone else. I was until I met you, but we can make this work."

"I'm so scared. I was wrong once. Seeing Craig again today only made me think about how wrong I was. I can't go through that again."

"I'm not asking you to." Gabriel stroked his fingers through her hair and brought her close to him, cuddling her head against his chest. "Do you hear that? That's my heart breaking."

The loud thumping sounded in her ear. The soothing touch of his hand riveted her attention. His scent of soap and pine engulfed her.

"I see that you have two choices here. You can embrace life with zeal or you can continue to hide and run away. Which is it gonna be, Rebecca?"

She heard the ticking of the clock on the wall as it echoed through the room, proclaiming her indecision. The stroking of his hand stopped, conveying his mounting tension. *Lord, I'm scared to risk my heart again. Help me.*

When her silence continued, Gabriel pulled back and stared at her. "I sign on, Rebecca, for life."

She opened her mouth.

"Mom! Mom!"

Peter burst into the room. Rebecca jumped away from Gabriel, feeling the heat creep up her face.

"Mom, come quick. Josh is standing on his own."

Everything evaporated from her mind except one thing—Josh. She hurried into the living room right behind Peter and came to a halt when she saw her youngest son taking a shaky step toward her grandmother. Stunned and in awe of what her son was doing, Rebecca froze, tears flooding her eyes and streaming down her face unchecked.

"Thank you, Lord," she whispered as Gabriel took her hand.

The feel of his fingers around hers, his arm touching hers, made the moment perfect. Josh stumbled, and before she could move to catch him, Peter whisked him up, laughing and shouting his joy.

"Who's my man? Josh is my man. I knew you could do it," Peter said, swinging his brother around and around.

Rebecca grasped Gabriel's other hand, compelling him to look from Josh to her. The tenderness in his gaze melted any doubts she might have had. "Yes, I'll marry you, Gabriel Stone. Name the day. I'll be there."

He grabbed her in a bear hug and swung her around, shouting his joy. When he placed her feet on the floor, he glanced over her shoulder at her grandmother and Peter. "Rebecca has just agreed to be my wife."

"This indeed is a wondrous day. Praise the Lord." Rose pushed herself to her feet and came to them.

Peter stood Josh next to him and slowly they made

their way toward Rebecca. When the pair was a few feet away, Gabriel scooped Josh up into his arms and faced Peter.

"Will you give your blessing?" Gabriel asked her eldest.

Rebecca held her breath. Peter liked Gabriel, but would he accept him as a stepfather?

A serious expression marked the boyish lines of Peter's face as he thought about Gabriel's question. Cocking his head, he finally replied, "Can I be your best man?" A grin split his mouth.

Epilogue

Breathing in the scent of pine always brought a smile to Rebecca's lips, but on this magical night, the scent reminded Rebecca yet again that she'd come home. Home to Gabriel. Home to the Lord.

At the end of the Reverend Carson's touching service, Alicia switched off the overhead lights, leaving only the softly wavering candle flames on the altar to light the sanctuary. Instantly, Rebecca knew what it must have felt like that night in Bethlehem. A dark, cold night when the cry of a newborn babe had been all it took to warm the people's hearts and souls, a cry that proclaimed a new beginning for everyone.

In the shadowy darkness, Rebecca rose with the choir to sing the last song of the Christmas Eve service. She looked at the sea of faces before her and felt a wealth of love and good fortune.

Gabriel, standing next to her, took her hand in his and gave her a reassuring squeeze. "You ready?"

"Yes, my love."

Tears of pure joy pooled in her eyes as she flashed him a brilliant smile. It seemed her whole life had been about this moment. He picked Josh up. She tightened their family's bond by taking Peter's hand, and with the four of them linked together, they moved as one to the front of the choir. Together, as a family, they sang "Silent Night." The singing was a gift Rebecca wanted to offer to the Lord for all He had given her. Gabriel's deep voice complemented Peter's and hers as they paid tribute to Christ. They finished the song with their voices blending as one, just as over the past months they'd blended as a family.

When the lights came on, washing the church in a rich brightness, everyone began filing out of the sanctuary. Gabriel didn't release Rebecca's hand. Instead he pulled her around so she stood in front of him, much as she had the day she had agreed to be his wife. He brushed a kiss across her forehead.

"Have I told you how much I love you today?" Gabriel asked, taking her other hand and holding them between their bodies.

She tilted her head and thought for a long moment. "Mmm—let me see. Nope, I don't think so. And you haven't missed one day since we married five months ago. My, Gabriel Stone, you seem to be slacking on the job."

He pulled her closer, laughter deep in his eyes. "You didn't hear me when you were waking up this morning."

"So that's what you were whispering into my ear.

I had other things on my mind. You know me first thing in the morning.''

He smiled, the lines at the corners of his eyes deepening. "Yes, I do. You're a touch grumpy, Rebecca Stone."

"You would be, too, if you were carrying around an extra ten pounds."

His eyes softened. He laid his hand on her rounded stomach. "You're exceptionally beautiful in the morning—in the afternoon—in the evening."

"You're just saying that because I'm carrying your child." His compliments never ceased to bring a full flush to her cheeks. She felt the love in his voice to the depth of her being and marveled that one man could make her feel so special and complete.

"Highly unlikely, since I've thought that from the first day I saw you."

"If you two lovebirds can quit cooing, it's time to cut the birthday cake for Jesus," Granny said behind Rebecca.

"Did you hear something, love?" Gabriel winked at Rebecca, his gaze never leaving her face.

"You know how sound carries in the church, Gabriel."

"Funny, you two. I know that Josh and Peter are hungry for some cake."

"Well, in that case, let's get a move on it. We don't want to be last in line for our piece of cake." Gabriel began ushering his family toward the door.

George McCall, with his sister and her three children, stood several people in front of them. Rebecca slipped her arm through Gabriel's and leaned against him, watching closely as he spied George a few feet ahead of them.

"I think it was wonderful that you talked to Ben about giving George a job," Rebecca said, slanting a look at her husband.

"Everyone deserves a second chance. I got one, thanks to you."

The love for this man flowed through Rebecca, expanding her heart to encompass all. "You have shown me what a family should be. You guided me back to the Lord and helped me to find my faith again. I love you, Gabriel Stone."

*   *   *   *   *

Dear Reader,

For many years I have worked with students with special needs. When I came up with this idea for this book, I felt as though God had given me a mission. This is a story to celebrate the beautiful children I've been fortunate to teach. Every day I go to work I'm the one who feels special because I get to teach them, prepare them for their future. They give me an appreciation of life and make me look forward to going to work. I thank God for giving me the chance to teach students with a zeal for life and an unconditional love for others.

I hope you enjoy this story of Gabriel and Rebecca and the blessings a child with special needs can bring to a family. I love hearing from readers. You can write me at P.O. Box 2074, Tulsa, Oklahoma, 74101.

May God bless you,

Margaret Daley

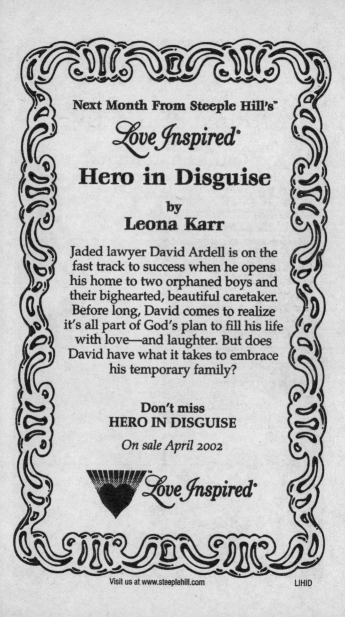

Next Month From Steeple Hill's™

Love Inspired®

Hero in Disguise

by
Leona Karr

Jaded lawyer David Ardell is on the
fast track to success when he opens
his home to two orphaned boys and
their bighearted, beautiful caretaker.
Before long, David comes to realize
it's all part of God's plan to fill his life
with love—and laughter. But does
David have what it takes to embrace
his temporary family?

**Don't miss
HERO IN DISGUISE**

On sale April 2002

Love Inspired®

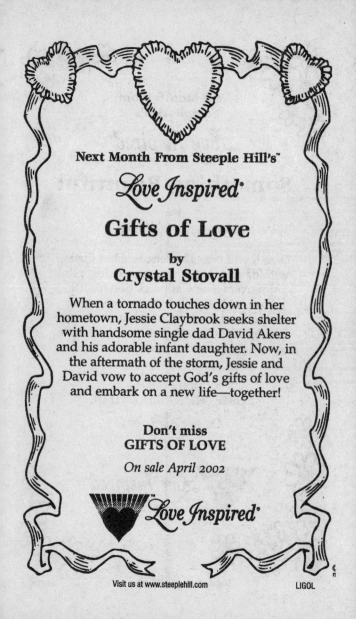

Next Month From Steeple Hill's™

Love Inspired®

Gifts of Love

by
Crystal Stovall

When a tornado touches down in her
hometown, Jessie Claybrook seeks shelter
with handsome single dad David Akers
and his adorable infant daughter. Now, in
the aftermath of the storm, Jessie and
David vow to accept God's gifts of love
and embark on a new life—together!

**Don't miss
GIFTS OF LOVE**

On sale April 2002

Love Inspired®

**Next Month From
Steeple Hill's™**

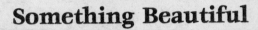
Love Inspired®

Something Beautiful

by
Lenora Worth

Daredevil Lucas Dorsette relishes flirting
with danger. However, the reckless pilot
discovers a new appreciation for life
when he falls in love with a stunning
supermodel who shows him the true
meaning of courage. But will their faith
help them face an uncertain future?

**Don't miss
SOMETHING BEAUTIFUL**

On sale April 2002